MY DREAM
LOVER

THE COMPLETE CYN CASTLE ROMANCE LIBRARY

My Dream Lover

Rainy Day Lover

Danny Boy

Nola

Eva

Rachel's Confession

MY DREAM LOVER

A Cyn Castle Romance

Cyn Castle

Published by Bancroft Mysteries, LLC

First published in 2005 by Renaissance E-Books
Second Edition (eEnhanced: new cover art and supplementary material) published in 2022
by Bancroft Mysteries, LLC
Mackinaw, IL 61755
www.BancroftMysteries.com

Cover design by: Tamian Wood
www.BeyondDesignInternational.com

ISBN 9781958521014 (Pbk.)
ISBN 9781958521106 (e-book)

Printed in the United States of America

*This book is dedicated to Arthur Oliveira,
for his support and encouragement
republishing this series.
Archie is a 'someone' who looks
at obstacles and challenges
in life and says,
"We can do this."*

CONTENTS

CHAPTER 1

"What's so wonderful about this guy?" Jan asked.

"He has thick, dark, wavy hair that cascades over his ears. He usually wears jeans when he teaches, and the denim around his backside is stretched as tight as a drum. When he talks, he sometimes raises an eyebrow. It's like a caress. It's nerve-wracking," Meg said while looking off into the distance.

"Meg, what's got into you? You're twenty-three years old. I thought you were immune. I worried that you'd wind up an old maid. You still could if you go after the impossible. I hear the girls in his classes all have the hots for him. You'd probably have to kiss his ass just to get him to notice you."

As it turned out, Meg did just that—and more.

❖ ❖ ❖

"If I get to babysit his daughter, he'll have to notice me. I saw the job notice on the bulletin board, called him, and I have an interview this afternoon."

"How can you save any money toward next semester on—what did the notice say—five dollars an hour?" Jan asked. "You can make more than that as a waitress. He's too old for you anyway."

"He's only thirty-one. I checked. I've got to get home and do my nails."

"You'll be making an awful mistake, Meg. Don't do it."

"Don't worry, Jan, he probably won't want me anyway."

The two girlfriends were in Gelding Junior College's deserted cafeteria. They were having a last cup of coffee at their usual table. They had earned two-year certificates, Jan in home economics and Meg in journalism. Jan was pregnant. Meg was going on to the University of Illinois at the end of the summer if she could raise the money.

"At least I'll get to talk to him."

"Okay, go home and do your nails. Don't be a stranger. I'll let you hold the baby. Love you, Meg. I've got to go."

The girls shared a quick hug, and Jan—Mrs. Jerry Turner, now that she was married—left. She was about to start a family while Meg's life was on hold. Jan and Meg had spent three fun years working their way to California and back after high school. Then Meg helped her parents move to their retirement home in Florida. She spent a couple of years dating guys she never really cared about, and now? Here she was back in central Illinois, with credit for two years of junior college, and plans to go to the university and get a journalism degree.

Meg filed a torn nail on her right little finger and glanced at the dirty dishes in the kitchen sink. She finger-combed her long brown hair.

"Damn it, Helen."

Her roommate, Helen Meyers, was nowhere around. She held down two restaurant jobs and spent most of her spare time with her boyfriend. She seldom did her share of the chores.

At least she paid her part of the rent. Meg couldn't afford to live there alone. Helen kept saying she was going to move in with her boyfriend. Where would that leave Meg?

After showering and applying lotion to her damp skin, Meg dressed in white shorts, a light blue sleeveless T-shirt, and high heels. She prodded her hair, then gave up trying to get the natural waves to stay put, applied a slight blush to her cheeks, and left for the appointment with Mr. Bradley Wayne.

Rose Moore Apartments was at the edge of Naperton, only a few blocks from where she lived. By the time she walked there, sweat had run down her back and into her shorts.

When she met Mr. Wayne—Brad—words she might say ran through her mind.

"Hello, I'm the silly girl who went gaga over

you when I took your class last semester. I want to be your babysitter, so you can get to know me. Really know me."

She wouldn't say that, of course. But what? She tried not to think about it. He wouldn't want her anyway. He'd probably be suspicious of a young woman interested in a babysitting job. Meg found apartment #201 in the second building of the complex, hitched up her shorts, ran her fingers through her hair, and pushed the doorbell button.

"Hi." Bradley Wayne opened the door and waved her inside. He held a cell phone to his ear. Meg stepped into the apartment and waited in the large living room, bare except for a worn couch, a large TV set, and a child's red chair and desk. There was no carpet.

He was well over six feet, a foot taller than her.

"Yes, Mother, I'll be careful. I've had several applicants. All of them are so young. It's hard to tell. I'll let you know."

He walked into the kitchen. Meg followed and noticed how his brows knitted when he frowned.

"You're Miss …?"

"Meg Collins. I'm here about babysitting. I called this morning, Mr. Wayne."

"Call me Brad, please. Coffee?"

"No, thank you. I don't drink. Well, I do like coffee, but not now. Thanks," she stammered.

"Sit down, please. I pay five dollars an hour. You

might have to stay overnight, even for several days. I'm a newspaperman. I never know when I'll be called out on an assignment. I have a six-year-old daughter, Hannah. I'm divorced. That's why I need a babysitter."

"I know," she replied.

"You know. How? I didn't say all that in the notice I put on the college board."

"I was in your class."

"Aha, that's the reason you look familiar. I had a babysitter, but she's moving away. I understand your parents live in Florida."

"Yes, they do. How do you know that?"

"Look, Miss Collins, I check a little on my students, and apparently, you did the same. Natural enough for a couple of snoops like us. So, we both know a little about each other. Why do you want the job?"

Because I want to watch, you put on—or take off —your jeans.

She turned away, her cheeks lightly flushed. What a thing to think. "Where is your daughter? I like children; that's why I want the job."

Brad stood and paced. Two long strides took him from one wall to the other. He turned and looked into Meg's eyes, holding her spellbound.

"I'm going to trust you to take care of my daughter. I've been worried about how young the other applicants were and whether they would be responsible. I can't figure out why you would want such a job. You were a good student."

Without thinking, Meg stood, started to pace, and stepped aside when Brad glided past her. She stood in the corner, away from his path.

"I'm saving money to attend the University of Illinois to get my journalism degree. You're a journalist. Maybe I could learn something from you."

"Okay. My daughter's at a friend's apartment here in the building. I'll have Brittany bring her down. I thought it would be best to have her out of here while I interviewed prospects. She's six years old, but I told you that."

Brad picked up the phone, mumbled something into it, and said, "Brittany will bring her right down."

Meg tried not to stare at his tight, faded jeans. It was just as difficult to avoid staring at the white T-shirt clinging to his chest and broad shoulders. That had all been interesting enough, but what took her breath away was the sight of his bare feet.

My God, she thought, struggling for air. *If his bare feet do that to me, what will happen if he takes off his shirt or pants?* Meg turned away and felt the heat in her face from blushing.

The front door opened, and a little girl in a ruffled dress hurled herself into Brad's arms. A sleek woman followed.

"Meg Collins, this is my daughter, Hannah," Brad said as he placed the child on the floor.

"Hello, Meg Collins." Hannah extended her hand. Meg bent to Hannah's level and shook her tiny hand solemnly. She smiled. What a perfectly adorable child.

"And this is Brittany Arnold," Brad said.

Meg straightened and came up a couple of inches short of Brittany, slender, immaculately coiffured, and manicured. Meg self-consciously smoothed wrinkles from her shorts.

"Got to get back to the office, Bradley," Brittany said before he could answer.

"Thanks, Brittany," Brad said.

"Thanks, Brittany," Hannah echoed.

The woman left without giving Meg another look. The new sitter sat on a kitchen chair and beckoned Hannah to sit on her lap.

"Brittany doesn't want me to sit on her lap," Hannah said.

"Why?" Meg asked as she adjusted the wiggling body to her contours. Hannah settled in and leaned her head against Meg's shoulder.

"She says it messes up her clothes."

Brad sat across from them at the kitchen table.

"Hannah, how would you like to have Meg stay with you when I'm working?"

"Do you know how to play checkers?" Hannah asked.

"I think so. It's been a long time, but I bet you could teach me."

Meg looked down into the child's blue-gray eyes like her daddy's. There the similarity ended.

Hannah was plump, like a peach, and her face was much too pliable to resemble his. Did Brad ever smile? Meg couldn't remember him smiling in class; he hadn't smiled since she'd been there, not even when he spoke to Brittany.

"What do you think, Miss ... er ... Collins? Do you want the job?"

Before she could answer, the phone rang.

"Damn," Brad said as he lifted the receiver and listened. His frown deepened.

"Couldn't you send somebody else?" he said. "Slatetown? What's the name of the school? I'll get back to you in a few minutes, Ed. Yeah, just give me a minute or two."

He hung up the phone.

"Oh boy, I get to go this time. You promised, Daddy, you promised," Hannah said excitedly. "My bag's all packed just like yours."

"I know I promised, kiddo, but ..."

"Oh, Daddy, please," she begged. "Meg can come and take care of me. You promised."

He looked at Meg.

"I did promise. I've been gone so much lately. An eight-year-old girl is missing. Hasn't been seen for two days. I had hoped I could take Hannah along on some routine assignment, but I can't take her to something like this."

"I could come along, take care of her."

"Would you? Are you sure? Your pay will start at once. We'll have to leave right now. It's about one hundred miles south of here, so we'll have to stay overnight. Ed says there's just one motel there. I should have told him to call and make a couple of reservations. We'll worry about that when we get there."

"Let's go," Meg said, surprising herself.

While Brad called his office and said he was on his way, Meg realized she would be without extra clothes and makeup—everything she took for granted. Still, she was excited to be going on an actual assignment with a real reporter.

Brad replaced the telephone receiver and nudged a pair of loafers from under a chair. He slipped his feet into them.

"I guess I'm not civilized yet," Brad said as Meg watched. "I hate to wear socks in the summertime."

Meg and Brad listened to radio reports on the missing girl as they raced south in Brad's two-year-old Escort. Hannah soon was asleep in the front seat. Brad didn't say a word as he drove and listened to the radio. It was comfortably cool inside the car, and Meg began to nod. She curled up on the back seat and was asleep when they arrived in Slatetown. Brad parked in front of a small motel. Weeds grew in the parking lot cracks, and paint was peeling from the front of the office. An electrical sign announced their arrival at the

GRAND MOTEL, EIGTEEN UNITS, AIR-CONDITIONED

"Meg, will you take Hannah inside, get a couple of rooms and wait until I get back? If you don't mind, buy something to eat. I'll repay you. I have to find the school."

As soon as they were out of the car, Brad sped away. Hannah took Meg's hand. In moments they were damp with sweat in the stifling heat.

"Daddy should have let us go with him," Hannah said.

"Maybe later. First, he wants us to get settled, so you'll have someplace to sleep tonight."

Hannah and Meg stood together for a moment inside the office, letting their eyes adjust to the semi-darkness. An old man sat behind a scarred registration desk, reading a newspaper. A musty stillness filled the place. The man paid no attention to Meg as she stood in front of the desk until she announced, "I'd like to rent two rooms for tonight."

His lower face was covered with gray stubble; the man wiped his mouth on his bare arm and focused his bleary eyes on Meg. "We got one room left. Reporters and photographers got all the rest. Came all the way from St. Louis and some even from Chicago."

"We'll have to take the one room, then."

Meg would be in a motel room overnight with Bradley Wayne. She turned to check on Hannah, who sat on a dark, worn couch, patiently waiting.

"Sign right here," the old man said. He pointed to a ledger laid open in front of her. Meg hesitated, then signed the book *Mr. and Mrs.*

Bradley Wayne.

"That's sixty dollars in advance," the man said. He seemed nervous. Meg felt he was asking for more than the going rate before the missing girl drew the media to town.

"My husband will be here after he covers the story at the school. He'll pay. We need to go to the room and clean up. Is there someplace close where we can get something to eat while we're waiting?"

"Didn't see any, did you? The nearest place is Miller's in town, but he's probably closed and hanging around the school like the rest of the sheep."

"Well, thanks anyway. Guess we'll just have to wait."

"There's some candy in those machines in the corner. Pop, too. The candy's stale, though. Can't go to the room until somebody pays."

"What?"

"Can't go to the room till I get my money. People run out on me before."

The girls each drank a bottle of root beer bought with the bit of change Meg had. It was a brand she'd never heard of, but it was rich and flavorful. Hannah made hers fizz by shaking it when the bottle was half-empty.

"So, you like to play checkers?" Meg asked. "Maybe they have checkers here."

Hannah jumped down from the couch and ran to the registration desk. The man was reading his paper again.

"Hey, Mister, do you have checkers?"

The man put down his paper, slowly got up from his chair, and came to the desk. He leaned over and looked down at Hannah. "Sure, I got checkers. Everybody's got checkers around here. I'm the champ; I don't care what old Elmer says. You want to play checkers?"

"I was going to play with Meg. She's my babysitter."

"Your babysitter? I thought she was your mother."

Meg felt like crawling under the couch when the old guy stared at her. He turned the ledger around, studied it for an instant, and said, "All right with you, *Mrs. Wayne,* if the girl and me plays a game of checkers?"

"Yes, of course."

The old guy pulled a board and a box of checkers from under the counter, opened the board, and asked Hannah, "Red or black?"

Hannah chose red and stood on her toes to see the board. Meg tried to concentrate on a gardening article in a dog-eared farm magazine. She heard a car pull up outside, stood, and saw Brad getting out. Meg rushed outside.

"There was only one room available. I signed for it as Mr. and Mrs. Bradley Wayne. The old fart at the desk wouldn't let us use the room until somebody paid. He wants sixty dollars. I only have ten."

"Come on," Brad said.

He marched up to the desk, pulled out his billfold, and presented a credit card.

The old guy, Mr. Jones, Hannah called him, looked at the card as though it were something evil. "Don't take no credit cards here. Cash does us just fine."

"Great," Brad said.

He opened his wallet again, examined the bills, took out three twenties, and gave them to Mr. Jones. "I'll need a receipt," he said.

"Everybody needs a receipt. Wear my hand out writing receipts."

Their unit was the farthest one from the office, number eighteen. There were two single beds close together, a bathroom, a couple of stuffed chairs, and a desk. A dresser took up most of one wall. Hannah jumped on the first bed and later started unpacking her little suitcase.

"We don't have time for that now," Brad told her impatiently. "Besides, we'll probably only stay one night—I hope. I'm nearly out of money, and there's no telegraph office in this burg." He paused to catch a breath.

"Come on. We'll drive into town, get something to eat, then I've got to get back on the story. They're still trying to get an organized search going."

"Daddy, I'm hungry," Hannah said as they piled into the car. "So am I, kiddo. How about you, er, Meg?"

He's having trouble remembering my name. I must be making some impression.

"Yes, I could eat something. The old guy at the motel said there's a restaurant, but he figured the owner would be at the school like everyone else."

"I know where it is," Brad said.

Brad drove to the school, parked, and told Meg to get some sandwiches. "Anything is fine with me and bring them back here." He took one of several notebooks from the glove compartment, eased his long legs out of the car, and gave her the keys. "The restaurant is straight south one block and left a couple of blocks. You can't miss it, I was told."

He shouted the last part over his shoulder as he ran toward the school.

"Which way is south?" Meg shouted.

Brad motioned. "You're headed south."

Not a soul was in sight as Meg drove on a narrow street lined by neat tiny houses and yards. The restaurant was just ahead with its empty parking lot. A large neon sign atop the square cement-block building said m_ller's.

"What should we get?"

"Daddy likes hamburgers with everything. Better get him two. I only want one, no onions, and I hope they have ice cream."

"I'm not sure I have enough money," Meg said.

She ordered three hamburgers with everything, another with no onion, two cups of coffee, and an ice cream cone.

"I only have ten dollars, so we'll have to drop something if it comes to more," she told the man who took the order. He looked enough like the man at the motel to be his younger brother. Beyond the counter, a large woman in a dirty apron repeated the order when the man shouted it. A lone customer sat at a table near the front window.

"You've got enough. The total is nine dollars and seventy-five cents."

"It's to go," Meg said.

"Suppose you're here because of the missing girl," the man said. The sizzle of frying hamburgers came from the kitchen. "We were going to close, go to the school, but I figure all those reporter people got to get hungry sometime. Sure is a mess of 'em."

Eventually, the hamburgers were placed in a brown paper bag with "the no-onion on the bottom" and the two cups of coffee on top. Hannah carried the loaded ice cream cone, stopping every few steps to lick it. Meg placed the sack in the car's back seat and rushed back into the restaurant to get several napkins. She handed two of them to Hannah, recommended that she be careful or she was going to spill her ice cream, and slowly drove back to the school.

A crowd had gathered around a man standing on a chair. He wore an official-looking star on a soiled vest.

"Is that a news conference?" Hannah asked.

"I think it must be. Let's go over to the swings. We can sit on them and eat our dinner. Your daddy will join us when he's through. I think he saw us."

Meg placed the sack near the swings, hoisted Hannah up into one, and wolfed down one of the hamburgers, worried Hannah would drop the cone before consuming it.

She managed to eat all of it and ate her hamburger as she held on to the swing with one hand. Meg nudged the swing with her hip while she sipped coffee and wished she had ordered two sandwiches. They finished eating, and Hannah urged her new babysitter to push her higher.

"Hang on tight now," Meg said.

"Yes, for heaven's sake, hang on, we don't need an accident here." Meg turned. A woman of about sixty walked to a swing beside Hannah, sat on it, and pushed herself back and forth with one foot. The woman had gray hair tied in a bun and sad, close-set eyes half-buried in a wrinkled face.

"Do you live here?" Meg asked.

"Yes, I'm Mrs. Stewart. Live across from the back of the school." She looked at Meg. "You here because of the missing girl? Are you a reporter?"

"No, not yet," Meg replied. "I'm babysitting for a reporter. This is Hannah, his daughter."

"What do you mean, not yet?"

"I'm going to school to be a reporter. Did you know the missing girl?"

The woman stopped swinging and squinted as she held a hand above her eyes. "They keep running off to the woods looking for Candice. But she's not out there. She told me she couldn't go into the woods because she got poison ivy. See that young woman standing beside the deputy, the blond one with all the makeup? That's Candice's mother. Some mother. She lets her kid run wild. I feed the kid half the time in the afternoon. Pretty little thing even takes a bath at my house sometimes."

Meg stood before the woman and put all the pleading she could muster into her eyes. "There's a notepad and pen in the car right there." She pointed to Brad's Escort. "Would you wait while I get them and then let me interview you?"

"Why?"

"Because you know the missing girl. What you have to say is important and exciting. Your name would be in the newspapers."

"Sure, honey, get your stuff. I'm not going anywhere. I'll swing missy while you're gone."

Meg dashed for the car, glancing over her shoulder every few paces to ensure Hannah and the woman were still there. What if this was a hoax so the woman could kidnap Hannah? She was breathing hard by the time she returned. The woman continued to swing Hannah as she answered the questions.

Her name was Violet Stewart; she was sixty-one years old, widowed, lived at 315 Sixth Street, and said the missing girl was Candy Anders.

The swish of Hannah's swing broke the silence as Meg scribbled what she hoped were legible notes, including the part about the girl and poison ivy.

"Have you told the authorities about the poison ivy?"

"Authorities? Ha! Do you mean Billy Wampler, the sheriff's deputy? He's so busy acting like a big shot he wouldn't listen to me. Besides, it serves Candy's mother right. Let her worry a little. It will make her pay more attention to the kid. She's divorced, working at some restaurant over in Clarkston, living in a trailer, and staying out all hours of the night. Sleeps all day. Let her worry some. I'll bet Candy's done more than her share of worrying, what with being left alone half the time."

Meg pushed her left hand toward Matilda to slow the flow of words until she caught up. "Do you have any idea where she might be?"

"All I know is last night I put a couple of ham and cheese sandwiches in a bag with a quart of milk on the back porch, and they were gone this morning."

"Where could she hide close to your house?" Meg asked.

"There's a tree house two houses down. The boys who made it have grown and left, but the thing is still there. It was nothing but a shack in a tree, but it would be a place to sleep. If she is staying there at night, I'll bet she has a blanket and everything. I hope she doesn't get in too much trouble because of this. I could be wrong. Maybe she's really lost, but I doubt it."

"I'm from Naperton, the *Daily Press*. We're supposed to have a photographer here by now. Would you wait until I find him so we can get your picture?"

"Sure, you just run off and find him, dearie. I'll watch the little girl here."

"No," Meg said hurriedly, hoping she hadn't offended the woman by her tone, but there was no way she would leave again without Hannah.

Brad finally showed up. Meg introduced him to Mrs. Stewart, told him about her notes, and convinced him to get a photo of her.

Gordon Mays responded to Brad's call by scurrying down the pole. He was up a utility pole shooting the crowd around the school. Mays appeared fat and inept, up close, like a clumsy teddy bear. Brad told him about Mrs. Stewart.

"Don't be too obvious. We don't want the rest of these vultures to see you shooting the woman. They'll know something is up."

Gordon Mays fumbled with his camera and seemed to fade away as he looked for something in a canvas bag suspended from his shoulder.

"Let me see your notes," Brad demanded.

He frowned like a parent looking at a bad report card as he studied them.

"I can just make them out. You wait here for Gordon. He can take the film to the bus station at Crankston and get it back to the paper in time for the morning edition." Brad walked into the school as if he had all day to get there. Minutes later, he was back.

"They've got a makeshift newsroom in the school library: computers, telephones, the whole bit. I filed the story and talked to Gordy. He'll take the film over to Crankston. Let's go back to the motel room, clean you up, kiddo, and get some sleep, okay?"

Hannah nodded. Fantasies danced through Meg's mind as she thought about the sleeping arrangements.

CHAPTER 2

T he beds in the motel room nearly touched. Brad separated them as much as possible without blocking the bathroom. By the time he finished, he was sweating.

"Guess we better turn on the air conditioner," he commented. He pulled off his T-shirt and pushed the start button on the machine. Nothing happened. He pushed it again and whacked the casing with the heel of his hand— still nothing.

"It doesn't work, does it, Daddy?" Hannah said.

Brad tried to open the one window, but it wouldn't budge.

Meg had given him an exclusive report with her interview of the woman on the swing, but her exhilaration evaporated as she collapsed in a chair and fanned her face with a hand. Beads of sweat rolled down her neck and under her blouse.

Brad avoided looking at her and opened the door. There was no breeze. "I'm going to the office to see if I can get somebody to fix the air conditioner or get the damned window open."

"Let's go with him," Hannah said. "We can get more root beer."

"You two go ahead. I'll sit here for a moment, then see if anything in the bathroom works."

* * *

In the motel office, the old man had no sympathy for their dilemma. "Well, I'm sorry. That air conditioner is busted, all right, and the window is nailed shut. People used to open the window and run the air. Had to stop that. You could leave the front door and the bathroom window open. It'll cool some after the sun goes down."

Brad resisted the urge to tell the old guy to take his motel and shove it, but he couldn't risk staying out of town if the girl was found.

"It'll be okay for one night, won't it, Daddy?"

"Right, kiddo. We'll manage it, won't we?"

"Yeah, we'll handle it, and Meg too, she'll handle it, won't she, Daddy?"

"I think she will. Do you like her?"

Hannah nodded as she drank from a soda can. Brad carried the other two cans and could not stop thinking of the perspiring woman in his motel room. They would lie practically next to each other all night, and Hannah would sleep soon after they cleaned up and ate. All the excitement of the day was sure to wear her out.

Then what? *Nothing, damn it, nothing.*

The sound of splashing water greeted them when they entered the room. Hannah put her soda can on the little table and ran into the bathroom. She was back in an instant.

"Meg is taking a shower, Daddy."

"I know."

"Can I take one with her, please, Daddy?"

Hannah had already kicked off her shoes, taken off her panties, and pulled her dress over her head.

"You better wait until she finishes," Brad said, but it was too late. He heard the shower curtain draw back, a startled laugh, then Hannah's laughter above the sound of the water. Lucky Hannah.

Brad tried to ignore the laughter, sipped root beer, and forced his mind to devise a plan. He would wait until almost dark, get Gordy and his camera, and watch the tree house where the girl might return.

Maybe Gordy could find the girl's mother, get some shots of her, and invite her to watch with them. Brad had told Gordy where he was staying and asked him to check in before he wandered off looking for a beer joint, a woman, or both.

Meg appeared in the doorway of the bathroom. She had put on her wrinkled clothes and rubbed her hair with a dingy towel.

"Wow, I feel much better even in these clothes, but I'm already sweating again. There isn't much hot water, maybe none by now. It's your turn if you want to take a shower."

Brad had watched while the towel obscured her eyes much of the time. He noted the slenderness of her legs and the fullness of her breasts, the sweep of her neck, and the depth of her warm, brown eyes once she had stopped fluffing her hair.

Spewing gravel and squeaking brakes quickly brought Brad to his feet. "That's probably Gordy."

Hannah bounced out of the bathroom, beaded water glistening on her naked body.

"Gordy's coming, kiddo," Brad said. "You better get back in there and put on something."

Meg put a hand on Hannah's shoulder and led her back into the bathroom. Brad watched. It was great to have someone taking care of Hannah. She needed a mother. Meg seemed perfect for the job, and she was showing definite signs of being a good reporter. He'd lose her come fall and probably never see her again. By then, it would be hard on Hannah.

Brad went outside and shouted at Gordy, marching toward the office.

"Over here, buddy," Brad said. "We've got to make some plans for tonight. You'll have to postpone your nightlife for a couple of hours. Did you find a place to stay?"

"Not yet. I'm working on it. Good work on the story. We beat the rest of the assholes."

Gordy shook Brad's hand.

"Not all my doing," Brad admitted. "My babysitter found the woman who knew the missing girl."

"Your babysitter. I take it she's inside with Hannah? I wish I'd known you were bringing Hannah—I would have brought her something."

As Brad opened the door, Hannah squeezed past a bed and hopped into Gordy's arms.

"Well, Miss Lollipop, I see you know how to dress for this weather. All of us should be so smart."

Hannah was wearing a pair of underpants, nothing else.

"Is that all right, Mr. Wayne? I didn't think there was any need to dress her until we went to eat," Meg said.

"So, this is your babysitter, Mr. Wayne. Should I call her Lollipop too?"

Meg stiffened. "My name is not 'Lollipop.' I hope your photos are better than your manners."

Brad laughed. He liked the spirit of this young woman more and more. Gordy appeared speechless.

"I didn't get a chance to introduce you earlier. Miss Collins, Meg, this is Gordon Mays, our speechless photographer. Meg, er, Miss Collins *is* Hannah's babysitter. She and Hannah are here because I'd promised Hannah she could go along on the next assignment. This happened to be it."

Brad saw the question in Gordy's eyes as

the photographer looked at the crowded motel room.

"We all stayed in this room because it was the only one available."

"Hannah and I just took a shower. The air-conditioning doesn't work," Meg added.

"So I noticed." Gordy wiped his brow.

"Put on some clothes, kiddo, and we'll all go eat," Brad told his daughter. "We can talk about tonight later," he added as he turned to Gordy.

"Where?" Gordy asked.

"That place near the school. Miller's. We don't have enough time to look for anything else."

They sat in a booth at Miller's and ate juicy hamburgers and french fries and drank milkshakes. Nearly all the booths and tables were filled. Conversations spilled over from one group to another, with the same common thread: the missing girl.

"I hope you don't eat like this all the time," Meg said to Hannah.

"Am I eating too fast?" Hannah asked.

"No, you're eating fine. Use your napkin. I mean, I hope you eat stuff that is good for you. Vegetables, fresh fruit, things like that?"

"We don't, do we, Daddy? We eat TV dinners a lot at home. Green beans sometimes; I hate green beans. That's vegetables, isn't it? Daddy makes me eat them."

Brad heard the conversation even though he was trying not to listen. He and Gordy discussed lighting for any photos that might be possible if the girl was in the tree house.

"I'll meet you there at eight," Brad said.

Gordy nodded, grabbed one more french fry, patted Hannah on the head, and left.

Meg gently used a napkin to wipe milkshake residue from Hannah's upper lip.

"You seem to have a way with children," Brad said. Heat flared for an instant on Meg's cheeks.

"We better get out of here. I've still got work to do. You two can read your book, Hannah, while I'm gone. You did bring it, didn't you?"

"It's in my bag. You said you would read it to me like you do at home."

"I did say that. But Meg will do it, won't you, Meg? I asked that old guy at the desk for a fan. Said the only two he had were in use. 'Don't even have one for me,' he said. It might help if we left the door open and opened the window in the bathroom," Brad suggested.

"I'm sorry I didn't give you time to get some clothes," he added to Meg. "I never thought of it. And this place, I'm sorry about it too, but what can I do? We'll be on our way home tomorrow, I hope."

Back at the motel, Brad went into the bathroom, stood in the tub, grabbed the handle on the window, and lifted it hard. The window slammed into the top frame. It was a wonder the glass didn't break. When he released the window, it closed with a bang. He went outside and found a stick to prop it up.

"That's about par for this place. One window is nailed down, and the other is so loose I nearly broke it. What's the matter with you two?"

Hannah laughed and pointed at his face. "You have dirt on your lip, Daddy. It looks like a funny mustache."

Brad grabbed Hannah, picked her up, and planted a kiss on her lips. He rubbed his face on hers.

"Now, young lady, whose face is dirty?"

Hannah jumped up and down on the bed. "Do it to Meg, Daddy.

Brad looked at Meg, shrugged, and said, "Can't do that, Hannah. All the dirt is gone now. It's all on your face."

"No, it isn't, Daddy. There's still some on you."

Brad said, "I've got to grab a quick shave. Going to leave the bathroom door open. Try to catch a breeze."

Meg collapsed into a chair and watched. His muscles flowed with each stroke of the razor. *What if he had kissed me, as Hannah suggested? Would I have wrapped my arms around him, let our sweat merge? What a thought! How will I get any sleep thinking like that? And which bed should I sleep in?*

Hannah brought the book and climbed into Meg's lap. Her skin was damp and warm because she was down to her underpants. It was too hot to be sitting like this, but Meg endured. She wanted to read to Hannah. Perhaps it would take her mind off the mountain of masculinity in the bathroom just steps away. Meg wished she could strip to her underpants. Maybe she would when Brad was gone. She certainly wasn't going to sleep in her clothes.

A hint of intoxicating aftershave caught Meg off guard when Brad came out of the bathroom. He carried a towel, maybe the same one she'd used. He wiped the moisture from his chest and arms. She thought of smelling the towel after he left, and Hannah was asleep. What a heathen thought. She would do no such thing.

"Well, kiddo, I've got to go. I don't know when I'll be back. You go to bed as soon as Meg finishes the story."

He leaned over and kissed Hannah, and his arm brushed Meg's. His face was so near that Meg could have bitten his ear. Her breath caught. He slowly raised his head. There was no need to smell the towel because his scent had already filled her. She looked away as he stood.

"You choose the bed you want, kiddo. I'll sleep with you. Meg can have the other bed, okay?"

She looked at Brad and nodded. She didn't trust herself to speak.

Hannah and Meg were yawning when they finished the tale of two dogs and a cat off on a long journey. Hannah begged Meg to sleep with her. She decided to lie down with the child until she went to sleep and then transferred her to the other bed.

She was asleep in no time. Meg lay on her back, watched the moonlight on the lower wall from the window, and yawned. Maybe she would go to sleep. She was tired, and her muscles relaxed as she drifted, then it was black, and she was trapped inside a small round space, like the bottom of a bottle.

She reached her tiny hands up and felt a small round opening. Her body became jelly and squeezed out of the hole like ointment oozing from a tube. She expanded as she popped out of the bottle onto a sandy beach. A palm tree waved gently in the breeze. Meg took a step. Countless grains of sand caressed her feet, sending pleasant sensations up her legs. She walked to the tree, turned, and leaned her back against it.

After raising her hand to the top of her head, she was in the kitchen of her childhood home. She measured up to the mark she'd made on the wall and was pleased to learn she was five feet, four inches tall. The kitchen disappeared, and she was again on the beach, dipping a toe in the cool water. The waves in front of her parted, and Brad emerged, getting taller with every step out of the water. He was naked. Her eyes raced up and down his body and fixed on his penis. It was soft and sort of floppy, but then it swelled. She touched it, put her fingers around it, and felt it grow as his arms wound around her shoulders.

His chest rubbed against hers, and for the first

time, she realized she also was naked. Her nipples became rigid. His penis throbbed just as her nipples did.

"Oh, Brad, I've waited so long," she said, but there was no sound. His lips moved as though he was talking, but there was no sound then either.

His left arm swooped between her legs, lifting her off her feet. Her crotch fit comfortably against the inside of his elbow, and her breasts rubbed against his chest. He carried her along the edge of the waves, each step causing her vagina to rub against his arm. There was a sound, like a cough.

Meg's eyes flicked open and stared into Brad's gaze. Her arms were wrapped around a pillow. She melted into his eyes for an instant before she felt heat rush her face. She was lying on her back with only a pair of panties and a wet T-shirt. She reached down for the sheet and pulled it over herself. He was in his shorts.

"Sorry I woke you. Guess you were dreaming. See you in the morning."

He eased his big frame into the empty bed. Meg turned away in case his penetrating eyes drew her to him. After a while, she slept, but the dream didn't return.

In the morning, she woke to birdsong and the sound of gentle rain.

* * *

Brad listened to the rain. He had been awake

for several minutes, perhaps longer. At first, he didn't move, afraid Meg would catch him looking at her. When he could no longer resist, he turned and held his breath as he stared at Meg's bare limbs as she lay on her back. He thought she was naked until he saw her panties as she turned. She was covered by a sheet when he returned from the bathroom.

Her face looked as innocent as Hannah's. She still was asleep, the hint of a smile on her face. Was she dreaming? What would a young woman like her dream about?

He knew what his ex-wife, Dorri, dreamed about, and it wasn't him. She was in California pursuing an acting career. He wished her success but, at the same time, wondered how she could abandon Hannah, her own child.

Now he was looking at this young woman, letting her attach herself to Hannah—no, that wasn't exactly right—Hannah was attaching herself to Meg. Either way, he had to be careful. He couldn't get involved with this young woman who would leave in the fall to pursue her ambitions.

Brad closed his eyes and thought of how the newspaper's front page—with his byline on it—would look with the story of how the missing girl was found in a tree house where she had been sleeping.

Gordy got nine or ten great shots of the girl and her mother as they embraced, tears and all.

He had raced back to Naperton and got there in plenty of time to get the photos in with Brad's story. It had been a successful assignment.

"Can we take another shower—can we, Meg?"

Hannah was awake, wide awake judging from her voice. Meg mumbled something. Brad imagined the sight of her. She had probably sat up, stunned.

Meg said, "My gosh, Hannah, you pulled all the covers off me. I'm practically … well, yes, I guess we can take another shower. We can close the bathroom door. It's not so hot now. You take clean clothes. I'll be right with you."

Brad lay on the bed, pretending he was asleep.

"Settle down, Hannah, please. You'll wake your father. He worked late."

Hannah came into view, and Brad closed his eyes. He opened them again just as Meg walked by. She dropped something and bent to pick it up. It was all Brad could do to avoid reaching out and grabbing her behind.

Once they were in the bathroom and the door was closed, Brad dressed hurriedly and drove to the bus station to see if the latest edition of the *Naperton Daily Press* had arrived. The bus station, a small cement-block building surrounded by a larger parking space, was closed. He sat in the Escort waiting. It was nearly six o'clock. Surely the place would open soon. It had felt cool when he first left the motel room, but now he was sweating again in the humid air.

It would be a relief to get on the road, head back to Naperton, and enjoy the car's air-conditioning. Maybe Hannah would want to sit in the back, and Meg would sit in front. They could talk. What about? There was her career. She'd shown promise. She didn't know yet that he had insisted her byline be included with his because of her contribution to the story.

The growl of a large motor shattered his thoughts. A bus rumbled into the lot and parked to the left of his car. The front door swung open, and a uniformed driver stepped out. He stretched, looked around, said hello to Brad, and added, "That damned George, he should be here by now. He's late half the time."

"I was waiting for a copy of the *Naperton Daily Press*. Do you deliver them here?"

"Yeah, I've got a bundle of 'em. If George doesn't show up in the next minute or so, I'll dump 'em and move on. There's more to my route than just this burg. Did they ever find that girl who was lost down here?"

"Yeah, that's why I'm here. There should be a story with photos in the *Press*."

The driver, a balding man, Brad noted once the guy removed his hat, also had a protruding stomach. He returned to the bus, wrestled a bundle of papers from one of the seats near the front, and plopped the bundle down near the front door of the bus depot.

The driver cut open the strapped bundle, and Brad picked up a paper. On the front page was a photo of the mother and daughter embracing. And then there it was, below a banner headline, his story ... and Meg's.

Strange how used to seeing his byline he had become. The thrill of getting the story intrigued him now, not the byline. But for Meg ... This had to be her first, except for school newspapers. He remembered the thrill of his first *Press* byline and wondered if she would be as excited as he was. Of course, she would. She wanted to be a journalist, didn't she? There was no denying the byline was a big part of it.

Brad left money for the copy of the paper, thanked the bus driver, and drove back to the motel. Meg and Hannah were outside doing bending exercises. Brad hurried out of the car and tossed the paper to Meg. She unfolded it to the front page. Her eyes glowed. "Oh, this is wonderful. They found the girl. Isn't that wonderful, Hannah? They found the girl."

"Look at the byline on the story," Brad said.

"Byline?"

Meg frowned, stared, looked at Brad with wide-eyed wonder, and whispered, "But how, why? My name with yours ... on the front page of the *Press*. It's incredible. Why?"

"Because you contributed to the story. You found the woman who led to our finding the girl. You broke the story."

"But I ... what did I do? She came to me while we were at the swings."

"You asked the right questions. That's the reason we got the story. And I'll talk them into paying you something too. Let's get back to Naperton. We'll celebrate with a royal lunch at a place of your choosing. Right, Hannah?"

"Choose McDonald's, Meg, please. I like to play there."

"Would you like to sit in the back seat, Hannah? Then, when you get tired, you can curl up and go to sleep," Brad suggested, hopefully.

"If you sit in the back seat, use the seat belt," Meg told her.

It was pleasant, speeding north on the four-lane highway, watching corn and soybean fields roll by. Meg pointed out cows and horses to Hannah, who said she wanted a pony.

"We should live in a house with a big yard, Daddy, so I can have a pony. Could you teach me how to ride it, Meg?"

Meg glanced over her shoulder at Hannah and laughed. Brad smiled to himself. He'd been lonely but hadn't wanted to admit it. Now the sound of her laughter, like chimes in a gentle breeze, filled him with domestic thoughts—thoughts of a mother for Hannah ... and a lover for him.

Another fifty miles, and Hannah was asleep.

"Want to get some music on the radio?" Brad asked.

"Not yet, please. I want to thank you again for the byline. You can't imagine what a thrill it is for me."

"Oh, I think I can. I'm not so old I don't remember my first byline. It wasn't on the front page; it wasn't even hard news. Just a little feature story about a guy who grew vines all over his house, his fence, everywhere." He paused for a moment. "What do you think? Do you want to work for me this summer, take care of Hannah?"

"Yes, oh yes. I love her already, and after that byline, I'll do anything you want."

"Really?"

"Within reason, Mr. Wayne, within reason."

"I've got to go into the office for a couple of hours, take care of some loose ends. How about if we stop at your place? You can pick up some clean clothes, and then we'll go to my place. You keep track of the hours so I can pay you, okay?"

"Thanks. I'll certainly be glad to get some fresh clothes."

Meg ran up the steps to the apartment building and let herself into the lobby. She took the elevator to the second floor. She knew something was different the minute she opened the door, even before seeing the note on the kitchen table. Helen, her roommate, had moved out. Now she would have to move. She could not afford to pay for the place by herself. Finding another roommate might take all summer. In the meantime, she'd be stuck with the full rent.

She couldn't afford to work for Brad. Two jobs would be needed just to have a chance to make it. Working odd hours for Brad at night would eliminate any chance for a second job. And what about Hannah? Meg already figured out how tough it would be for her and the little girl when she left for the university. Meg hadn't figured on it being this soon, but maybe it would be better.

CHAPTER 3

"I 've got to talk to you, alone, when we get back to your apartment," Meg said when she returned to the car with a small suitcase.

"We can talk alone now if you like; Hannah's asleep. If I know her, she'll sleep while I carry her to the apartment and put her to bed. Something the matter?"

Brad started the car but didn't move it.

"My roommate has left; she went to live with her boyfriend. I hope it works out this time, but I can't afford the apartment alone. Even if I worked two jobs, I couldn't afford the apartment and save enough money for school. And I couldn't work two jobs if I had to be on call when you were sent out of town or on a night assignment."

Brad pulled the car away from the curb and drove slowly to his apartment. As he predicted, Hannah remained asleep while he carried her to bed. She sighed once she was in bed, stretched, rolled over, and wrapped her arms around her pillow.

"She's such a sweet girl. I'm going to miss her."

"She'll miss you too. It's obvious that she needs someone like you. Dorri broke Hannah's heart when she left."

"And yours too?" Meg asked and regretted it as the words escaped. "I'm sorry. I shouldn't have asked."

Brad had his back to her while making coffee. He turned and looked beyond Meg. "It's okay. It wasn't the greatest thing in my life. Her leaving, then the divorce. I suppose it's for the best. Dorri wouldn't have been happy. I soon realized she didn't want to be tied down as a mother."

"Thanks." Meg accepted the cup Brad handed to her. They sat at the kitchen table, and Meg absently rubbed a finger over the new red Formica top.

"It's the only new furniture I've bought so far," Brad said. "Would you consider living here? There are two bedrooms, of course. You could sleep with Hannah. No rent. I'd pay you for eight hours a day. Would that give you enough for school?"

He knows. He knows I was praying he would offer that very thing.

"I'm not much of a cook, but I could learn. Hannah and I could learn together. She'd love cooking supper for you."

What am I saying? Do I really want to live in the same apartment with a man who stirs the most primitive emotions within me? A man who would only have to flick a finger, and I'd be in his arms? Of course, I do.

"Wouldn't it be awkward, us living together? I mean, well, you know."

"You don't have to worry about me. I've had it with women; I mean the romance stuff. You can depend on it, and I wouldn't bother you."

You already bother me, you oaf. And what about me? I suppose you're saying I don't bother you. I won't bother you if that's how you want it.

"What do you think?"

A dark cloud raced in the sky as Meg stared beyond Brad through the kitchen window. The smell of fresh coffee filled the kitchen. He sat across from her, his eyebrows raised in that peculiar way that she imagined was effective when asking questions to get a story. What did she think? She shouldn't appear too eager.

"We could try it, I suppose. I love taking care of Hannah, and I would be able to save enough for school. I guess we could try it."

"Good, then it's settled. This evening I'll take you back to your apartment to pick up the rest of your clothes and you can give your notice. I've got to get to the office. Kiss Hannah for me when she wakes up. She'll be thrilled when she learns you're going to live here."

Meg stayed at the kitchen table after he left. Hannah would be thrilled, he'd said. She was thrilled—but Brad wasn't. He was satisfied he'd solved his babysitting problem.

* * *

Brad raced down the stairs instead of taking the elevator. His major worry was over, at least for the summer. He'd always managed.

Getting someone to look after Hannah whenever necessary had been a hassle. He could have sent her to his mother in Florida. She would have loved to have her, but Brad didn't want to think about being apart from his daughter. She must never think he didn't want her. She'd had enough of that with Dorri. He'd never dreamed what being a father would mean. Dorri might be able to forget her responsibilities as a parent, but it was something he couldn't and didn't want to do.

Now? The problem was solved for the moment, wasn't it? Or would he ruin the setup by getting involved with this warm, vibrant young woman Hannah already seemed to love?

At the office, work took over, although the image of Meg sleeping in the motel room popped up uninvited now and then. She'd be in the apartment when he got home. Maybe she and Hannah would have supper ready. He looked forward to eating in the apartment instead of dragging himself and Hannah to a quick food place or, God forbid, eating another TV dinner.

He was sitting in city editor Ed Grange's office. Ed's neatly trimmed mustache was bobbing. He leaned back in his leather chair. "So, Brad, tell me more about this woman you insisted deserved a byline. How did she earn it?"

Brad formed the facts in his head, thought of the most efficient way to explain them, and told the story.

"She's my babysitter now. She's going to the University of Illinois in the fall to complete her education. She'll be a good one, I think."

"Why don't we hire her for the summer then? Let her get her feet wet. Maybe she'll like it here and come back when she finishes school. We get some of our best people that way."

"Yeah, I know. I thought of suggesting that, but, damn it, I need her. I feel guilty about not suggesting it to her. Hannah likes her. It solves all of my problems for a while."

"Lucky you," Ed said. "A man with all his problems solved. Nice work on the missing girl. Take the rest of the day and tomorrow off."

❋ ❋ ❋

Meg had plenty of time to think as Hannah slept. She could save money for school. She loved being with Hannah, but would she be able to keep her feelings from Brad? He'd think she was a fool.

Hannah came into the kitchen, rubbing her eyes. She climbed onto Meg's lap and announced she was hungry. Meg poured a bowl of Toasted

Oats, the only food she found.

"Is this your favorite kind?" Meg asked.

"No," Hannah said. "I told Daddy to get the one with the tiger on it, but he forgot. This is the first time I ever ate breakfast food for lunch."

Hannah went to the refrigerator, got milk, poured it, then returned it to its place and ate the cereal with a soup spoon.

"What could we do today that would be fun while your daddy is at work?"

Hannah chewed a spoon full of cereal. "I know, we could go to Bloomington Park. They have swings, flowers, a zoo, and picnic tables. Could we go on a picnic, go to the zoo, do lots of fun stuff?"

"We sure could," Meg agreed enthusiastically.

She had less than ten dollars, money she had picked up at her apartment. Would it be enough? Hannah hurriedly ate the rest of her cereal, raced into her bedroom, and dressed in what Meg imagined was record time. "Your socks don't match," Meg commented and pointed to Hannah's feet.

"Oh my. Thank you. I did that before and didn't notice it until I was in school. It was awful."

Meg smiled. Hannah could be such a grown-up little girl one moment and the child she was the next. Meg's heart swelled. Only a couple of days ago, she was jealous of her friend Jan because she was going to have a baby. Meg still wanted a family of her own, but for the moment, she had a little girl to look after. She couldn't have Brad, but at least she had Hannah.

"Do you think we should leave a note for your daddy? He didn't say when he would be home."

"Let me write it, please."

Hannah left the kitchen and returned with a box of crayons and a piece of paper. She sat poised, ready to write.

"What should I say?"

"Just tell him we went to the park."

Hannah frowned and pressed hard on a red crayon as she scrawled in crooked letters, *Daddy*. She looked up at Meg, her brow furrowed in concentration. "I guess you'll have to write the rest, Aunt Meg. Can I call you Aunt Meg? I call Brittany aunt, but I don't think she likes it."

"Yes, of course, you can call me Aunt Meg, or just Meg, whatever you want."

Meg scrawled in letters like Hannah's, *Went to the park*. "Okay, let's go. How do we get to the park?"

"We can walk. Daddy and I walk there sometimes."

Meg had looked through the cupboards and refrigerator while Hannah was eating. There was little food in either place and nothing suitable for a picnic. Meg decided not to bring up the question of food until later. Maybe there was a stand at the park where they could buy hotdogs or something.

Hannah was still going strong after a couple of

hours of swinging and sliding. She skipped and hopped beside Meg as they headed for a shaded picnic table and bench where Meg could rest her weary legs.

"It's a nice day, isn't it?" Hannah said.

At the picnic bench, Meg stretched her legs and sighed. She turned her face upward, looked at the blue, unclouded sky through the tree leaves, and agreed it was indeed a nice day. She realized she was hungry. She'd have to do something about feeding them but hadn't seen a food stand in the park. Where could they get something, anything to eat?

The question still was on Meg's mind when she spotted Brad striding across the grassy expanse between the bench and the swings. He carried two brown paper bags. Hannah shrieked as her father waved. Meg's heart fluttered, holding her hand to her chest for a moment. It was the first time she'd seen him smile.

"I read your note, Hannah. I didn't know you could write."

"I only wrote 'Daddy.' Aunt Meg wrote the rest."

"Oh, and here I thought you wrote the whole thing."

He carefully placed the sacks on a nearby picnic table, turned, and opened his arms. Hannah jumped at him. He caught her and raised her above his head. As he lowered her to the ground, she shouted, "Do it to Meg, Daddy, do it to Meg."

Heat rushed to Meg's face, but Brad didn't look at her. "I hope you guys are hungry. I brought hamburgers and french fries. Some soda, too."

Hannah chattered between bites. After a long silence, Brad looked toward a group of children playing across the park and said, "It's a nice day for a picnic."

"Yes," Meg replied. "Hannah and I were just saying the same thing."

After they finished eating, Brad got up. "You can take a break now. I'll take Hannah to the zoo. You haven't been there yet, have you?" Before Meg could answer, Hannah shouted, "Meg gets to go, Daddy. I want to show her the little bears. Please, Daddy."

"Well, sure, kiddo, if she wants to go. I just thought maybe you had worn her out by now."

Meg felt like a tree, maybe one of the elms that dotted the park, as Hannah and Brad discussed her as if she weren't there. The poor trees stood by while people played and talked all around them, never being included—*poor me.* Hannah ran ahead. Meg was about to shout at her not to cross the street by herself when she pulled up and looked back.

Meg worked to keep pace with Brad. He turned, noticed she was slightly behind, and waited until she caught up. "I talked my city editor into paying you one hundred dollars for your part in getting the story yesterday. It should be more; it'll be a while before you get the check.

Everything has to clear through the business office."

"Gee, thanks," Meg said, surprised. "I never expected that."

Brad picked up the pace again. Hannah grabbed his hand, waited for Meg, and grabbed her hand as well. Hannah skipped between the adults as they crossed the street.

* * *

Brad sat on a bench across from the girls as they laughed and gestured to each other while watching two woolly bear cubs wrestle and tumble.

The mother, a giant black bear, seemed to ignore the cubs, but Brad knew she would be all growl and teeth if anything threatened them.

Brad imagined Meg would be the same way if anything threatened Hannah. He felt such relief, having a dependable babysitter. And yet, he realized he was on edge. It was that damned sex thing. He had to try to ignore her, or she would see he was fascinated. If he could keep her from realizing that, maybe he could avoid complications. Maybe she would simply tell him "no" if he did make any advances. He couldn't do that anyway. An employer had no right to impose himself on an employee.

As they climbed into Brad's car, Meg said, "If you want me to cook dinner, we'll have to get some groceries. All I found for Hannah's lunch was breakfast food."

"Yeah. We've been eating out. I don't know anything about cooking except I warm up a mean TV dinner. Are you sure you wouldn't just rather eat out tonight? I'll leave some money; you and Hannah can go grocery shopping tomorrow. Okay?"

"Let's do it tonight, Daddy; let's do it tonight."

"No, kiddo, you can do it tomorrow. There's a grocery store only a couple of blocks away. We can eat at the usual place tonight."

Hannah ordered a hamburger and french fries at a table near the Downtown Cafe's front window. The waitress, a teenage girl with pimples and dark-rimmed glasses, devoted her attention to Brad. "You know better than that, Brenda. Give Hannah the meatloaf special or the roast beef. Which do you want, Hannah?"

"Oh, Daddy, do I have to? The meatloaf, I guess."

Brad ordered the roast beef and sighed. It was good to relax after such a long day. By the time they got home, the sun would be setting, and Hannah would go right to sleep. He and Meg could have coffee and watch the sunset through the apartment's picture window. He had watched it alone so much lately. It would be good to share it with someone. He'd have to give her first rights to the bathroom. Maybe he shouldn't do that, though. Dorri used to take hours to get ready for bed. If Meg were that way, it'd be damned late by the time he got to take a shower. Maybe he'd just wait and take one in the morning.

He was right about Hannah. She didn't protest at all when he suggested she go to bed as soon as they entered the apartment.

Meg helped Hannah take a bath.

Left alone, Brad sat in the cushioned chair, drank a cup of coffee, and watched the sun slide below a cloud and disappear behind a high-rise building. It was pleasant to sit there, knowing Hannah was well cared for, that someone else was sharing the responsibility. The female chatter died, the lights were turned out, and Brad was sure Hannah was already asleep.

Light from the kitchen cast a long shadow into the living room. Meg sat in the chair beside him, a glass of water in her hand, and sighed.

"I see I missed the sunset," she said, disappointed.

"It was a good one. Lots of pinks and blues with the sun's rays turning some of the clouds into fire. I thought I'd let you have the bathroom first. Do you think you'll be able to sleep okay with Hannah? She rolls around some. She crawls into my bed some nights."

"I'm tired enough I could sleep on the floor. Why don't you use the bathroom first? I need to just sit for a while. It's been quite a day."

Meg thought she might fall asleep in the chair.

She had slumped down and extended her feet to the floor. There was a clatter of things, shaving equipment probably, from the bathroom. The toilet flushed, silence for a few seconds, and then the sound of the shower.

No chance of sleep now. She imagined Brad in the shower, with her pasted behind him, washing his back. She imagined water cascading down his chest, the soap suds sliding down his length. How wonderfully crowded it would be.

The sound of falling water stopped. Meg heard the swish of the shower curtain as it was pulled back then Brad was standing beside her. He was rubbing his hair with a bath towel. A red and white striped bathrobe covered his body to the knees. His feet were bathed in light from the kitchen. Meg stopped breathing. Her chest swelled until she thought it would burst. The air rushed from her when it could be held no longer.

"The bathroom's all yours. I'll see you in the morning. You don't have to worry about an alarm clock. Hannah will take care of that."

Meg went into the bathroom, let her clothes drop to the floor—probably where Brad's had dropped—stepped into a warm shower, and caressed her body with the same bar of soap he had used. And he was just a few feet away in the next room.

This has got to stop, she told herself. It didn't. She thought of Brad as she eased down next to

Hannah and dreamed of him while she slept.

Later Hannah's smiling face, eyes glowing, was close to Meg's.

Hannah giggled as she tickled Meg's nose.

"What time is it, Hannah?" Meg mumbled as the girl turned away. "I don't know, but the sun's up. Let's go in and wake Daddy."

"I've got a better idea, Hannah dear; let's go back to sleep."

"Aw, please. Daddy wakes up funny. Sometimes he grabs me and growls like the big bear at the zoo. It's fun."

"That's just between you and your daddy. I guess I might as well get up. I'll make some coffee and see what time it is."

Meg slipped into her robe, a faded blue chenille thing. She sucked in her stomach and tightened the belt to make her waist look as thin as possible. She fussed with her hair in the bathroom that separated the two bedrooms. Meg thought of putting on a little makeup but decided that was just too much. It was only her ego causing her to wear makeup at any time. She certainly wasn't going to start wearing it this early in the morning—Brad or no Brad.

She had just given up on her hair when a low roar followed by a peal of laughter erupted from the bedroom. Brad was awake. Meg walked past his bedroom and caught a glimpse of his bare legs. Was it possible he slept in the nude?

"Aw, coffee," Brad said later as he came into the

kitchen carrying Hannah on his shoulders. He'd had to bend his knees to get her through the doorway without banging her head.

He was wearing a pair of dress pants and an unbuttoned white shirt. His hair glistened, and waves merged into each other like an incoming tide. His feet were bare, and Meg looked away.

"Don't worry about fixing breakfast for me this morning. I'll grab something on the way to work. I see there's enough breakfast food for Hannah and you."

He took a billfold from his back pocket, counted fifty dollars, and put the bills on the table.

"Here's enough to get some groceries: something to cook tonight and whatever. You'll have to make a list of things we need. Hannah will help you, won't you, kiddo? She has definite ideas about what should go on a grocery list. Don't let her talk you into too much stuff that isn't good for her."

He stood by the kitchen counter, sipped his coffee, then drank the rest in two gulps. "Good coffee," he said.

He was out the kitchen door but returned to say, "Oh, how did you sleep? Did Hannah keep you awake?"

"No, not Hannah. I slept fine, I think. I don't remember. Guess I must have slept okay."

"I'll be back about four or four-thirty."

He was gone. Hannah jumped down from the

kitchen chair she had been standing on, raced out of the kitchen, and returned with a pencil and paper.

"I know some good stuff we can put on the list."

"I'll bet you do. And you're going to tell me all about it, right?"

Meg picked Hannah up, hugged her, set her on the chair, and said, "Your breakfast is ready. Eat, and then we'll make a list."

While Hannah ate her breakfast, Meg started her latest diet by eating a piece of dry toast.

What did Brad like for supper? Hannah wasn't much help. She said hamburgers and french fries.

They started the list, and Meg hoped to impress Brad by making chicken cordon bleu for dinner, a recipe she hoped she could remember. Maybe there would be a cheap recipe book at the store, or else she'd have to buy things with cooking instructions on the package. Why hadn't she paid more attention when her mother tried to teach her to cook? Maybe some of it would come back. Meg had been like Brad and Hannah, eating junk food and stuff that came in a box.

"I get to push the cart," Hannah declared as they left the apartment building. She took Meg's hand and led her to a row of carports behind the building. A small plastic grocery cart was in the corner of the one marked for Brad's apartment, along with a tricycle and a rusted wagon.

Meg followed as Hannah pushed the cart and stopped to wait at each street crossing. Low gray clouds floated in a darkened sky. Meg wondered what she and Hannah could do all day if they were confined to the apartment. For one thing, they could dust.

Hannah raced ahead as soon as they entered Kensington Grocery Emporium, three blocks from the apartment. She turned into the cookie and candy aisle and tossed items in the basket without consulting Meg. When Meg caught up with Hannah, they retraced her steps, and Hannah reluctantly replaced most of the cookies and crackers she had grabbed.

"Now, kiddo, you go slower, and we stick to the list, at least for the most part. I'll let you choose a couple of things that aren't on the list before we leave. We can't buy everything in the store; the cart is too small."

Meg thought fifty dollars was more than enough, but she spent thirty of it for only three sacks of groceries. Two of them fit into the cart, and she carried the other. It was misting when they left the store.

Her blouse clung to her chest by the time they entered the building, and Hannah's hair was plastered to her face. In the lobby, Brittany Arnold stood aside to let them pass. Hannah stopped and said, "We grocery shopped. I got to buy some chocolate cookies, my favorite kind."

"That's nice," Brittany said. She nodded as she

pointed her pale pink umbrella at Meg's chest. "When it rains like this, a person's clothes might as well be a second skin, don't you think?" Brittany raised her chin a notch higher and walked out, her high heels clicking as she opened the umbrella before the door closed.

Hannah drank a glass of milk and ate two chocolate cookies. Meg resisted joining her. Her desire to lose at least five pounds won out.

"I'll show you how to dust, kiddo, and you can do that while I put away the groceries. Maybe, if it keeps raining, you can teach me how to play checkers. Okay?"

Meg rinsed broccoli, shook off the excess water, and placed it in the refrigerator. She had the chicken breasts, ham, and Swiss cheese, everything she needed.

During the afternoon, they played six games of checkers by a strange set of rules Hannah created as the games progressed. Meg would have to change that. She couldn't let the child think the rules could be changed whenever it pleased her.

Meg fussed with the meal preparations while Hannah took a nap. After flattening the chicken breast fillets with a jar used as a rolling pin, she breaded them, stuffed them with ham and Swiss cheese, and put them in the refrigerator, ready to cook.

Later she scrubbed Hannah clean, helped her get into a "Sunday" dress, and helped her comb her hair. Meg wore a snug blouse that did nothing to hide her female attributes, a flounced skirt, and a ruffled apron. They waited. Hannah was anxious to tell her daddy they would have "cord-on-blue," and Meg was nervous about how it would come out. Brad called and said he would be home by five. He was having a drink with some of his buddies from work. He said it was something he hadn't been able to do for a long time because of the necessity of getting home to take care of Hannah. He asked if Meg minded, but what could she say? *Yes, dear, I mind. You get home to your ... what?*

By six o'clock, Brad still wasn't home, and Hannah was hungry. Meg cooked enough "cord-on-blue" for her, and Hannah asked for seconds.

At seven, Meg gave up waiting, cooked all the food she had prepared, and told herself Brad would just have to eat it cold if he came home at all. What had she gotten herself into? Brad had shown every sign of being a devoted father. Surely, he wouldn't turn out to be unreliable and leave all the responsibility to her. She wasn't ready for that. And what about the end of the summer? What would happen to Hannah then?

Hannah was putting together a picture puzzle featuring a large duck, and Meg was eating when Brad arrived. He slammed the door, said "oops," and came into the kitchen, looking like an overgrown boy who'd continued to play outside after his mother called him home for supper. He picked up Hannah and twirled himself and her around.

"You smell funny, Daddy," Hannah complained.

He placed her back in the chair as carefully as if she were a fragile doll. He turned to Meg and said, "I'm sorry I'm late. The time just got away from me."

"Your food is cold; you'll have to warm it up," Meg said as she picked up Hannah and left the kitchen.

CHAPTER 4

After Hannah was tucked in, Meg read to her from Uncle Bob's Fables. Hannah was asleep before the first chapter was finished. Meg slipped out of the bedroom, started for the kitchen, hesitated, and went into the living room. She pulled the cushioned chair in front of the window, kicked off her shoes, and stretched her legs. She watched the sunset.

There wasn't much to see. The sky was still dark with rain clouds. Occasionally, a ray of sunlight found a crack in the cloud cover, creating a spectacular burst of color for a few moments.

Meg heard the microwave running in the kitchen. Brad must be warming up the food. How would it taste warmed over? Not as good as it did for her and Hannah. Served him right.

Later she heard water running and the clink of dishes. She was nodding despite herself.

"Why are you sitting in the dark living room?" Brad asked.

"I was watching the sunset, what little there was of it," Meg said.

"You have a right to be angry with me, I guess. As I said, the time just got away. Before, when I was married, I hung around with people from work and had a few drinks. I haven't done that since Hannah was born. As soon as she could, Dorri returned to her theater groups, leaving me to take care of Hannah."

"I had a reliable babysitter I could call for a while at a minute's notice. She was here when I was teaching that class you took. She moved away, and I've had a hell of a time since. It was such a relief not to have to hurry home. I'm sorry," Brad said as he blew his nose.

Meg shifted in her chair and turned to face him. The little light that was left glistened in his eyes. Was he crying?

Meg wiped the moisture away from her cheeks.

"Why should you be apologizing to me? I'm the babysitter. If I was angry, it was because of Hannah. She had been looking forward to eating 'cord-on-blue' with you."

The corners of Brad's lips turned up slightly. "'Cord-on-blue,' huh?" he said.

"You can sit here in the dark if you like. Do you mind if I turn on the television? I want to listen to the news channel. Oh, by the way, that 'cord-on-blue' was perfect. I ate all that was left, the broccoli, too."

"I didn't know what to fix. Do you have any favorite dishes? I could try to cook them, but I'm not promising anything. Here, you can have your chair. I'll go clean up the kitchen."

Brad stood and strode to the television. After he switched it on, he turned. "You don't have to worry about that. I did it. We can try to find something you want to watch after I listen to the news. Would any of your favorite programs be on now? And you keep the chair. I'll buy another one tomorrow, or maybe a couch. Want to help shop for it?"

"Well, yes, I guess, but Hannah would love it. No doubt she'll have ideas about what you should buy."

It was eleven o'clock before they went to their separate beds. They watched part of a movie featuring a love story about a prince and a farmer's daughter. That night, in Meg's dreams, Brad was the prince, but Brittany was the farmer's daughter.

Some farmer's daughter, parading around in Sunday clothes with not a strand of hair out of place. Meg was some sort of maid. Brad, the prince, came into the barn, and she curtsied. He said, "What are you doing? You shouldn't bow in front of me like that, with no bra and that sheer blouse. You might as well take off all your clothes."

Even in the dream, she knew he didn't mean that, but she ripped off her blouse and unfastened her skirt. It drifted to the floor.

"My God, you're beautiful," Prince Brad said. Meg really was dreaming. The next thing, she was on her back in the barn loft. Hay itched against her

skin. Prince Brad stood over her head, one foot on either side. She grabbed his ankles and gazed up to his long legs, past his bulging calves and knees, up the inside of his thighs to his erect penis. She tried to lift her head toward it, but he pushed it down gently, turned so his kissable butt was visible, and everything went dark. End of dream? Meg tried but failed to return to the dream.

Hannah again served as an effective alarm clock. She was seated at the kitchen table by seven, waiting for breakfast. The coffee was perking, and bacon was frying.

"Go ask your daddy how soon he'll be ready for breakfast, please."

Hannah was back in an instant. "He says he's ready now. He was combing his hair."

Meg caught a glimpse of Brad as he leaned against the kitchen doorway. Hannah was standing on a chair near the stove. Meg warned her of the dangers of splattering grease, then guided her hand as she scooped up the eggs with a spatula and placed them on a plate. Only one yoke broke.

"Smells good," Brad said.

"I helped, Daddy," Hannah announced proudly.

"So I see." He was talking to Hannah, but his eyes locked into Meg's. Meg wore beige slacks and a tan blouse covered by a fluffy apron. She certainly was overdressed for breakfast.

"You two look like an ad hawking domesticity," Brad said.

"What's domest ... what you said?" Hannah asked.

Brad sipped coffee. "Ummm, good. Domesticity is 'the good life,' I guess," Brad answered.

With short steps and a high degree of concentration, Hannah walked across the kitchen carrying the plate filled with eggs, bacon, and two pieces of toast and placed it in front of him on the kitchen table.

"Thank you, young lady," Brad said. He smiled, and Hannah curtsied.

"Where did you learn to do that?" Meg asked.

"On television. I saw it on the Disney Channel."

Brad dug into his breakfast. It could be good, this domestic thing, if ... How long would she be satisfied just being a babysitter? What about her ambition to be a journalist?

And what about Brad? Meg wondered. When she was pissed because he was late, he seemed to cringe.

"I'll try to get home about four this afternoon. We can go shopping for a used couch. I'm not ready to invest in new stuff until things get more permanent," Brad said. "If there is any reason I can't be here by then, I'll call. Okay?"

"Okay, Daddy," Hannah said.

Meg didn't reply. He watched her, that frown of concentration on his brow. She wiped her lips with a paper napkin and smiled. He looked away.

* * *

Brad sat in a chair as they examined the three couches available at Al's Used Furniture. The store filled about half of what had been an abandoned warehouse. The laughter echoed as they talked and took turns sitting and lying on a brown couch that appeared in better shape than the other two. Meg had changed clothes and was wearing a short skirt.

Hannah said, "Can we buy it, Daddy? Can we?"

"It's a good one," Al said, a bald, short man with a mustache. Brad handed him two twenty-dollar bills.

"You could get it upholstered, be just like new. I can deliver it after six o'clock today if you like. That's when I close."

They were eating supper when Al knocked on the door and asked if Brad could help carry the couch into the apartment. When it was inside, Brad and Hannah discussed where it should be placed while Meg cleaned up the kitchen.

Done at last, she joined them in the living room. Brad was sitting in the chair, looking out the window. So Meg sat on the couch and sighed. She stretched out on her back on the sofa and tugged down her skirt as far as it would go.

Meg turned her head and looked at Brad. He was still looking out the window. It was as if they were a longtime married couple, like her parents. Together, but each living in their own world. She was dozing when Brad said, "Well, that's enough silence for the day. Want to watch television?"

"No, thanks. I'm about to go to sleep. It won't bother me if you watch it."

"I feel like a psychologist, you on the couch, me sitting in the chair. Maybe I should start asking you questions."

"Fire away, but don't be disturbed, Doctor, if I fall asleep."

"Why do you want to get into journalism?"

"The usual reasons, I guess. The excitement of being involved with the day's news. Meeting interesting people, places you get to go."

"Very good. Let's see, what should I ask now?" Brad said in an attempt to imitate Dr. Ruth.

"I hope you don't start on Dr. Ruth's favorite subject. My sex life is not worth discussing."

"And why is that, my dear? You are young, attractive, and intelligent. Why is that?"

Meg sat up and tugged her skirt down again.

"I haven't met the right guy yet. And besides, I want to finish college before getting married and all that."

"My dear," Brad said, "you should lie down. How can I help you if you don't lie on the couch?"

"That is the worst imitation of Dr. Ruth I ever heard," Meg criticized when she stretched out again. She cut short her laughter when it occurred to her that her "boss" might not like being teased.

"Enough of this foolishness, young lady. This is serious. We must get at the root of this problem. Why do you hate men?"

It was only a game, yet she was concerned. She didn't want Brad to think she hated men, especially him. If only he would get out of the chair, get down on his knees, kiss her, and join her on the couch.

"What is it you are thinking? Tell Dr. Ruth."

"Sorry, Doctor, but I don't know you well enough to reveal my secret thoughts. Maybe at a later session."

"Okay," Brad said. "Perhaps it is too soon. See my secretary to arrange another appointment."

He got up and turned on the overhead light and the television. After the news, Meg went to bed and lay awake, wondering what Brad would be thinking. Probably something to do with his job.

Sometime during the night, one of Hannah's flailing arms woke Meg. After waiting for Hannah to settle down again, Meg sat up. Her mouth was dry. She slipped out of bed and went to the bathroom. There was a light under Brad's bedroom door. *He must be reading*, she thought as she hurriedly drank a glass of water and returned to Hannah's bedroom. Meg didn't want Brad to see her in the sheer nightie that just went past her stomach. Or did she? Once, she awoke with her arms around Hannah. She slept through it all.

Hannah and Brad were eating breakfast the following day, and Meg was waiting for the toast to pop up when the phone rang. Brad said his usual "damn" and asked Meg to answer it. "I don't want to talk to anyone this early," he said.

When Meg answered the phone, a woman's voice demanded to know who she was. "Perhaps I have the wrong number," the voice said. "I was trying to call Brad Wayne."

"You have the right number; I'll get him."

Brad took the phone, explained that Meg was his babysitter and after a brief conversation said, "It's Grandma, Hannah; she wants to talk to you."

Hannah's face lit up with a touch of egg yolk, adding color to the smile. She chattered away with her grandmother.

Meg felt embarrassed because most of the conversation was about "Hannah's babysitter."

"That's my mother. Sorry, but she's very protective of her granddaughter. She wants to be sure you're taking good care of Hannah. I tried to assure her, but she wants it from the subject's mouth."

"When?" Hannah shouted.

"Oh, gee, we can really have fun. Next week! How long can you stay? Is Grandpa coming?"

"Don't hang up, Hannah; I want to talk to your grandmother." Brad did little talking and a lot of listening.

"Of course you're welcome. It's just such a surprise. I'll pick you up at the airport then. Bye."

Hannah wiggled in her chair. "Grandma is fun, Meg, you'll see. She buys me lots of things." Brad seemed lost in thought.

"Anything the matter?" Meg asked.

"No, not really. It's just that Dad isn't coming. She said something about them wanting to get away from each other for a while. Don't know how long she'll stay."

Meg's mind was in a whirl. *Where will Brad's mother sleep? What will she think of me living in the apartment full-time? She'll think Brad and I are having an affair. I'll have to be especially careful how I conduct myself. No, damn it, I won't. Despite my thoughts and dreams, I've been conducting myself as correctly as anyone could. I don't need to apologize to anyone.*

I'm being unfair. I haven't even met the woman, and I'm already thinking of reasons to dislike her. How can I dislike someone so close to Hannah?

❋ ❋ ❋

"We'll work something out," Brad said that night as if he'd read Meg's mind.

"It is beautiful, isn't it?" Meg remarked thoughtfully, changing the subject. "I never really noticed the sunset before. And each night, it's different. A different arrangement of clouds or no clouds, different shades of pink, orange, red, and combinations beyond counting. Listen to me; I'm getting poetic."

Brad said, "I'm getting aches and pains from trying to hold Hannah steady so she doesn't wake up. She's growing so fast."

"Let me lift her off your lap. I'll put her to bed." Meg knelt in front of Brad. Her chest rubbed against his knees as she worked her hands and arms under Hannah. Her cheek brushed his as she lifted Hannah off his lap. For an instant, their gazes locked. Meg stood with Hannah in her arms. Breath escaped from her lungs as she breathed again.

"Is something the matter?" she asked after putting Hannah to bed. "You seemed to be far away all during dinner. I suppose tuna and noodles aren't all that exciting."

"What? Tuna and noodles. Oh, it was fine. I've been thinking of the complications involved when my mother arrives."

"What do you mean?"

"Well, for one thing, where will she sleep? They would probably have stayed in a motel if Dad were coming, but now ..."

"Maybe I should stay at a motel. How long is your mother going to be here?"

"I wish I knew. Don't misunderstand. I love her. Dad, too. They have been wonderful parents, and they adore Hannah. It's just that she won't understand."

"What won't she understand?"

Brad turned to look at Meg, and she smiled.

"Oh," he said. "I thought you were serious. You *know* what she won't understand."

"You mean she'll think we are sleeping together, take showers together, do it on the kitchen table, all that stuff?"

Brad stood and paced.

"She'll be concerned about how anything we do is affecting Hannah. She'll see right away how Hannah already loves and trusts you. Her main concern will probably be the same as mine."

"What is that?"

Brad stopped in front of Meg, then stepped back. "How Hannah will handle it when you leave to go to school. She went through that once when Dorri left. She's recovered now, I hope, but she'll have to go through it again. Who knows how the mind of a child works? Will she understand?"

"I think the thing to do is start preparing her now. I'll tell her of my plans to go to college in the fall, why I want to do it, and how she'll go away to college when she's older. She'll understand. She's a wise little girl."

"I hope. In the meantime, what do we do about my mother?"

"How about if I sleep on the couch? There is no sense in trying to hide the fact I live here. Hannah will tell her in one way or another. We don't want to ask her to lie, do we?"

"No, we don't. You are right. How did you get so smart?"

"I'm not smart yet, I'm just in training, so I'll be as good as you are at this journalism business."

* * *

Meg wiped off the kitchen table for the third time, cleaned the salt and pepper shakers again, and tasted the coffee. Brad's mother would be there any moment. Brad and Hannah had gone to the airport an hour ago. Maybe the plane was late. They should be here by now. What would Mrs. Wayne think of the apartment, of her?

Meg heard their voices in the hallway before they opened the door. She nervously smoothed her apron one more time and poured a cup of coffee. When they entered, she stood at the kitchen doorway, leaning slightly against it for support.

Brad put a large suitcase down and said, "Meg, this is ..."

Hannah raced up to her, took her hand, and pulled her into the living room. "Grandma, this is Meg."

"My, aren't you pretty, and such a pretty apron," Mrs. Wayne said.

"Thank you, and I'm pleased to meet you. Mrs. Wayne, Hannah has told me so much about you."

"I'm afraid she might be a little prejudiced in

my favor. And please call me Mary. She's been chatting about you and the fun you two have had."

Mrs. Wayne—Mary—sat on the couch and fanned her hand in front of her face.

"I'm surprised it seems so warm up here. I know. It's not the heat; it's the humidity. I'm exhausted. Would anyone mind if I nap right here on this couch?"

"I'll get you a pillow, Grandma," Hannah said. She raced into her bedroom and returned with a pillow from her bed.

"Thanks, dear," Mrs. Wayne said.

Meg went to the kitchen, poured her coffee into the pot, stirred it, and poured it back into the cup. She sighed. Mary seemed like a nice person. There were questions in her eyes, but compassion, too, and there was no doubt she loved Hannah, and Hannah loved her.

Her hair was white, her tanned face wrinkled, but there was a twinkle in her eyes, like the hint of one she'd seen in Brad's eyes. But Brad didn't look like his mother. Perhaps he resembled his father more.

"The flight was delayed for nearly an hour," Brad said as he sat across from her. After moving it carefully up to the table, Hannah sat in the other chair. She was quiet so her grandmother could sleep. She whispered when she talked and drank her milk without making a sound.

"We only have three chairs," Meg said. "Why

didn't I think of that?"

"Don't worry, Meg," Hannah whispered. "We can take turns."

"Yes, we can." Meg pushed one of Hannah's curls in place. "After your grandma naps, we can start supper. Maybe you should nap so you won't be too tired to help."

"I won't be too tired."

"Hannah," Brad said.

"Oh, all right, I'll lie down, but I just know I won't go to sleep. If I do, you promise to wake me when you start fixing supper?"

They promised.

"Would you like a cup of coffee, Mrs. Wayne?" Meg asked when Brad's mother came into the kitchen after only fifteen minutes.

"I can get it, dear, and please, call me Mary."

"Perhaps you two would like to talk while Hannah is asleep," Meg suggested. "I could go for a walk. I've been in most of the day. I'd enjoy a walk. It looks like it might rain." She realized she was rambling.

"You don't have to walk in the rain just because I'm here," Mrs. Wayne said.

"It isn't raining yet. I just thought ..."

"Brad and I will have plenty of time to talk later. Besides, he doesn't talk that much, just like his father. I can probably get more out of you than I can him. You know how mothers are. We always want to know much more than is their business. For instance, how did you two meet?"

"Brad ... er ... Mr. Wayne advertised for a babysitter on the junior college bulletin board. I answered the ad."

"You're a student, then."

Meg answered, saying she was and wondered if the next question would be: *Aren't you a little old to just be in a junior college and babysitting?*

"I started college late. My friend and I bummed around for a year and drove to California. Then I helped my parents retire to Florida. Stayed there for a couple of years. I finally got around to getting an education. I want to be a reporter. That's why I was interested in babysitting for Brad ... er ... Mr. Wayne."

Mrs. Wayne laughed. "Do you two really call each other Mr. and Miss when I'm not here? Sounds so formal."

Hannah came into the room, rubbing her eyes. She went to Meg and put her arm around the babysitter's waist. "I'm hungry."

Mrs. Wayne watched. Was she jealous because Hannah came to Meg first? Meg was about to suggest Hannah sit on her grandmother's lap when Mrs. Wayne spoke up. "Brad, why don't you and Hannah go to the store, get some pork chops, potatoes, and green beans? I'll make your favorite supper. Meg and I can talk while you're gone."

Brad looked at Meg. Meg said, "We don't have pork chops or green beans. I didn't know they were your favorites. We have plenty of potatoes.

Better get more bread, though."

They were gone in a few minutes, and she was left with Mrs. Wayne and the inquisition she knew was coming.

CHAPTER 5

"We saw your name with Brad's on a story about that missing girl. We get the Naperton Daily Press mailed to us. How did that happen?"

"It was quite a surprise and thrill for me. I had just started working for Brad. It was the first day, in fact. He had promised Hannah she could go on his next assignment, and to keep his promise, he took me along to take care of Hannah. He shared the byline, he said, because I interviewed a woman who knew the missing girl. It was kind of an accident."

"We get the paper so we can keep up on Brad a little and some of our friends who still live here. We just thought it was someone new at the paper. The byline with Brad's, I mean. I never dreamed it would be his babysitter. I suppose Hannah was thrilled when she got to go along."

"Oh, yes. She loved it. Hannah played checkers with an old man who ran the motel and met the woman I interviewed. Yes, she enjoyed it."

"You stayed in a motel?"

Uh-oh, I never should have mentioned that.

"Yes, the girl still was missing when we got there. She wasn't found until the next day."

"I see," Mrs. Wayne said.

Meg had trouble thinking of Brad's mother as anything but Mrs. Wayne. Still, she had asked to be called Mary, so Meg intended to try.

"How was your trip, Mary?"

"Nothing special. Uneventful, I'm happy to say. I can't say I much enjoy flying. We could have driven up if Brad's father hadn't been so stubborn. He said we would be interfering. If I know him, he'll call in a couple of days and say he's driving up, so I won't have to fly back."

"How is Brad doing?" she continued after a pause. "I mean, he took it so hard when Dorri left. So did Hannah. Is she okay, do you think?"

"Hannah seems fine. She's such a lovely little girl. We've had fun doing things together. It's a joy taking care of her. Brad seems to be okay."

Mary poured herself another cup of coffee. "Does Brad like this? Seems a little strong."

"He's never complained. Maybe I should ask him."

"No, don't do that. I always say that if a man isn't complaining, leave well enough alone. Are you two sleeping together?"

Meg stiffened. "I sleep with Hannah," she replied, trying to keep the anger out of her voice.

"I know it's an impertinent question, but I warned you I want to know what's going on. I'm worried about Brad and Hannah. Brad probably is on the rebound. You seem like a nice girl. I'm grateful for that. I was afraid some irresponsible woman would snag him while he was defenseless. Be a terrible thing for Brad as well as Hannah. Now, I'm worried about you. Does Brad know how you feel about him?"

"What do you mean?"

"Come, girl, I can see. You're in love with him, or you think you are. If Brad is just on the rebound, he'll come out of it, and you'll be left holding an empty bag. And what about Hannah? She shouldn't have to go through another separation from someone acting as a mother substitute."

Meg got up from the kitchen table and looked out the window at a cloudless sky. She hesitated before turning. "Yes, I am in love with Brad, but he doesn't know. He still cares for Dorri, I think. And he doesn't seem interested in me. I'm not going to seduce him if that's what you think."

"Now, don't get angry. We can be friends. I have a right to be concerned about my son and granddaughter."

Meg sat down again. She searched for the right words when Hannah raced into the kitchen with a bag of groceries.

"I want to help fix supper," she announced.

"And you shall," Mary said, "but slow down. You'll run right out of your shoes."

Brad came in, also carrying a sack of groceries.

As soon as he sat them down, Mary shooed him and Meg out of the kitchen.

"You can have the night off, at least from preparing supper. You and Brad can do the dishes. I'm afraid this little one will have worn me out by then."

In the living room, Brad planted himself in the chair and turned on the television to CNN. Meg sighed and sat on the couch. Her nerves relaxed like springs, with the tension slowly removed. Surely the worst was over. What more could Mary ask?

During a commercial, Brad glanced at her. "I guess you survived the grilling I'm sure Mother conducted. She's nothing if not frank. She used to ask me some personal, embarrassing questions when I was younger."

"She is direct."

"Did she ask you if we were sleeping together? Damn, I knew she would. I guess I should have warned you. I'm sorry."

"Don't be. Maybe it's a good thing. It's a natural enough question for a mother to have. Most mothers wouldn't have the nerve to ask it. Now it's out of the way if she believed me," Meg said.

"What did you say?"

"I told her I don't sleep with you until I'm sure Hannah is asleep."

"Sure, you did. I can see you're still a little annoyed. Like I said, I'm sorry."

Pork chops and green beans. Nothing to write

home about, Meg figured. *Ah, but I was wrong. The way Mary cooks pork chops and green beans makes them delicious.* They discussed the way the food was prepared while they ate. Brad said nothing, and Hannah even ate her green beans.

"Meg's going to sleep on the couch, and I get to sleep with you, Grandma," Hannah said after eating the last bite from her plate.

"Oh, I hate to rob Meg of her bed," Mary said. "Brad, why don't you sleep on the couch? Meg can sleep with Hannah, and I'll sleep in your bed."

"It's okay with me," Brad said.

"You'll be so uncomfortable. You're much too long for that couch. I'm shorter," Meg argued.

Hannah offered to sleep on the couch, but Meg insisted she wouldn't mind. "How many chances do you get to sleep with your grandmother? You can keep her awake with chatter as you did me the first night."

"I'll do the dishes; you and Brad must have lots to discuss," Meg offered after the meal.

"I think we've pretty much discussed everything," Brad concluded. "Hannah, you entertain your grandma while Meg and I do the dishes."

"You wash, I'll dry," Brad said when his mother and Hannah left the kitchen.

They worked in silence.

Brad's arm occasionally rubbed against Meg's as they worked. A dish crashed to the floor.

"Sorry," he said, "it slipped out of my hand. I'll clean it up."

The dish had broken into three main pieces, but shards scattered about. As he stooped to pick them up, Meg bent over to get the wastebasket from under the sink. She stood quickly, realizing the view of her rear she was presenting.

"I'm sorry if Mother embarrassed you with her personal questions," Brad apologized again.

Silence. What could Meg say? She'd already said the questions were okay. And, of course, the questions only served to whet her imagination for images of her and Brad in the most personal of situations—showering together, wrapped in each other's arms, kissing everywhere. She had to stop thinking like that, especially when he was nearby.

"You didn't really tell her we wait until Hannah's asleep before we sleep together, did you?"

"Of course not," Meg said. "You know I was only joking."

"Yes, but I can't help thinking of her reaction if you had said that. It would serve her right if someone were just as frank with her as she was with them."

"Yes, maybe. But I had nothing to be frank about."

Brad was silent for a moment. "I guess I should start dating again. Brittany keeps inviting me to things, but I've always wormed out of it. Now, how will I get out of it with you here?"

"Maybe you should go with her, get away for a night or two. It might do you good."

"Yeah, you're probably right. I've been mooning about Dorri for too long. A young woman at work has tossed a few hints, but that's not so great either. Fellow workers and romance can lead to all sorts of problems."

He was thinking of romance, at least exploring the subject a little, but he didn't include Meg in any of his plans. Why should he? She was only the babysitter. He could go out and ... damn him, while she stayed home. Meg knew she had no right to be angry but couldn't help herself.

"What about you?" he said. "Anytime you want to go out, I'll be happy to stay home and take care of Hannah. You ought to at least go to a movie or something. I never thought to ask. Do you have a boyfriend? He could come here for supper if you like?"

"He's in Florida."

Why did I say that? Because that was the last time I went out on a date? I avoided dates to stop fooling around and get serious about my education.

"Actually," she confessed, "there's no boyfriend in Florida. I'm trying to concentrate on my studies."

"Can't do that with a boyfriend, I suppose," Brad said. "I've got a box of journalism and related books somewhere. Maybe in the basement. There's a storage space down there for each apartment. I'll try to find the books if you're interested. It might save you some money this fall. I graduated from the University of Illinois. I guess I didn't tell you that."

"No, you didn't. We should talk about that if you don't mind. You could give me some tips on classes to take, that sort of thing."

"I'll find the books first. They'll refresh my memory, maybe. It'll beat talking about sex. Of course, I think about it, but I don't want to date anyone just yet."

"Me neither."

＊ ＊ ＊

Later, after Brad went to his room and Meg could see the light coming from under the closed door, she wondered if he was having as much trouble going to sleep as she anticipated she would. They had skirted the subject of romance, a subject constantly in the back of her mind. But apparently, he wasn't interested, and indeed, if he was, his plans didn't include her. Meg decided she'd be relieved when the summer was over. She'd hate leaving Hannah, but it would be good to get away from Brad and move on with her life. Eventually, she'd meet someone who would admire and love her, not just use her as a babysitter. She tossed and turned on the couch for what seemed like forever. When Hannah shook her, sunshine was slanting across the living room floor from the kitchen window.

"Wake up, Meg. We can fix breakfast for Grandma. I could do it by myself, but Daddy made me promise never to turn on the stove. We should fix eggs, bacon, and toast. I don't know how to make coffee."

"What time is it?"

"I don't know. It's morning," Hannah said.

Meg rubbed the sleep from her eyes. The light blanket she had covered herself with was on the floor. Had Brad got up during the night to use the bathroom and seen her in nothing but her nightie? He probably wouldn't have paid any attention anyway. She intended to help Hannah fix breakfast for the child and her grandmother, not for Brad.

Meg watched Brad yawn as he entered the kitchen. He mumbled hello to his mother and her, sat down, and sipped the coffee his mother had placed before him.

"I was sleeping, having a pleasant dream, when some little monster pounced on me, shook me awake."

As he talked, he looked at Meg. She looked away. "Does anyone here know where that monster went?"

Hannah giggled and shook her head.

Mary said, "I hope you two slept as well as I did. Even Hannah's tossing didn't bother me much. Did you manage to sleep okay on the couch, Meg?"

"Like a log," Meg replied. Brad still was gazing at her, and she wished he would stop. His mother would surely notice and draw some conclusion or other.

Breakfast was finished, and Meg was doing the dishes when the phone rang. It was a man asking for Mary.

"It's your granddaddy, Hannah; want to say hello?" Mary said after she talked for a few minutes.

Hannah babbled about all the fun she and Grandma had and returned the phone to Mary. Mary listened for a moment without comment. "We can talk about that when you get here. Drive carefully, and don't try to make the trip in one day. Love you, too."

After she hung up, she looked at Meg. "He's driving up, starting tomorrow. I knew he would. Silly old fool. We might just as well have come together, but no, he had to do it his way."

Brad came into the kitchen from the bathroom with a towel around his neck. Meg looked away to keep from admiring the flow of his chest muscles. His bare arm brushed against hers as he placed a cup in the dishwater. Meg leaned against the sink. She was sure Brad's mother was aware of the electricity sending tingles throughout her body.

"Your father is coming. He wants to know if it would be okay to take Hannah back to Florida for a couple of weeks. He doesn't want to stay away from his fishing buddies too long, but he wants to see Hannah."

"Can I go fishing too?" Hannah asked.

"Yes, I suppose," Brad said. "Two weeks, huh? I guess it would be okay if Hannah wanted to go. I don't suppose you want to go, though, do you, kiddo?"

Hannah climbed into her grandmother's lap. "He's just kidding, Grandma. He knows I want to go," Hannah said.

"I know. I'm his mother. I knew your daddy when he was just a little boy. He liked to visit his grandmother too."

"Who was his grandmother?"

"Well, she was my mother, but she's passed on. Someday you'll understand such things. Let's go make the bed, shall we?"

Brad poured himself another cup of coffee.

"Earlier, they wanted to take Hannah for the whole summer. I didn't want her to be gone that long. I guess two weeks won't be too bad. I shouldn't be so selfish anyway. She'll love it. And the trip and seeing Florida will be educational."

"Yes, of course," Meg replied. "It does present a problem for me. You won't need me. I can stay with a friend who is about to have a baby. She'll be glad for the help. But there won't be any money coming in. I'll never save enough to go to college this fall."

Mary came back into the room. "Isn't it about time you went to work, or are you a banker now?"

"It is; I'm late already," Brad said.

He hugged his mother, kissed her forehead, and shouted goodbye to Hannah. He glanced at Meg. "We can talk later."

"He means about my staying with a friend while Hannah is gone. I'll have to find a job to earn money while she's away. I need it to pay for college this fall."

"Oh, I'm sorry. I never thought how taking Hannah would create a problem for you. I thought that not having Hannah to care for might induce Brad to get out and find himself a good woman. He's been sulking about that no-account Dorri long enough. She was pretty, but I don't understand how she could leave Hannah, no matter how much she wanted to be an actress."

"I've wondered the same thing," Meg said

Meg cleaned, dusted, rearranged the dishes in the cupboard, washed all the dirty clothes she could find, lamented that she didn't have more clothes when she ironed some of the most wrinkled, and still it was only early afternoon. Mary had taken Hannah to see a Disney movie.

Brad got home before they did.

"Nothing much was going on today, so I got away early. I've been worried about this business of you leaving while Hannah is gone. Do you have to do that? I know there won't be much for you to do, but we could set up a study schedule or something. I hired you for the whole summer. I don't want to shortchange you."

"I don't think I could do that. What would your mother think of us living here alone while Hannah was gone? Besides, wouldn't it be dangerous?"

"Dangerous? Oh, that," Brad said. "We're adults; surely we can control ourselves. I hope I can."

Meg stamped her foot like a petulant child. "I can control myself too, Mister, but you aren't stupid enough to think nature won't be trying to take its course. I suppose I'm not that attractive. There wouldn't be any temptation looking at it from your angle. Only I would be tempted because of your magnificent build, your knowing gray eyes, your—oh, hell. Just forget it. I'll stay with Jan; maybe I can find a two-week job at a quick food place."

"Hey, whoa," Brad said. "I didn't say you weren't attractive. As a matter of fact ... But you're my employee. I would be wrong to take advantage of you. That's all I meant."

Mary and Hannah came into the apartment before Meg could respond.

"We'll talk about it later," Brad whispered.

Hannah lugged a shopping bag decorated with images of pink and red piglets. She pulled three dresses and a pair of bib overalls from the bag and held them above her head.

"Look what Grandma bought me, Daddy. And she let me pick one out. I liked the overalls. Lots of girls wear them at school. The rest are pretty dresses with ruffles and stuff. Like the ones Mommy used to wear."

They were gathered in the kitchen, where Mary was already making coffee.

"Why don't you let me finish that, Mary, and I'll cook supper tonight. Your turn to rest. You must be tired, trying to keep up with Miss Dash here."

Mary sighed. "You got that right. I won't fight you for the kitchen tonight. Thanks, Meg."

Brad, Hannah, and Mary went into the living room. Hannah asked them to sit down. "I'm going into my room to change, and then I'll model the clothes. Like they do on television. Okay, Daddy?"

Meg looked out the kitchen window as she began preparations for supper. She hoped the small roast in the refrigerator would be large enough for the four of them. She'd have to ensure everyone else had plenty of meat before serving herself. It was a beautiful late afternoon outside. The sky was blue again. It would have been an excellent day for jogging or going swimming. She had to find time to get back to that. The chatter and applause from the other room tempted her to look in. But should she?

When supper was served, everyone praised the roast, the hash brown potatoes, and French peas. Meg almost believed them. She was beginning to get a feel for cooking.

Two days later, Brad's father arrived bearing

gifts for Hannah, a kiss for his wife, and a handshake for Brad. Then he and Brad laughed and hugged each other.

"I hear you've given up rooting for the Cubs so you can spend all your time fishing," Brad said.

"I still do both. No matter what your mother says, I don't spend all my time fishing. I just thought it would be good for her to come up here on her own, get away from this old coot for a few days."

"You're the one who wanted to be alone."

"Brad, introduce your father to Meg."

"Oh, of course. Dad, this is Meg. She's taking care of Hannah this summer. She's a journalism student. Going to the University of Illinois this fall."

"She lives in," Mary said.

"Boy, you sure know how to pick 'em, Brad. First that looker Dorri and now this beautiful young lady. Meg. I like it. I like you. I'm a good judge of people, you know."

"Yeah, Dad, you must be. You chose Mother, or did she choose you?" Brad asked.

Meg's anger started to rise when Mary pointedly said she "lives in." Before it could heat up, Brad's father's remark about Brad knowing how to pick 'em wiped it out.

"Call me Herm, short for Herman. I hate Herman," Brad's father said.

"Do you have to leave so soon, Dad?" Brad said when his father announced two days later that he wanted everyone ready to leave by six the next morning.

It was closer to seven by the time the car was loaded. Meg had intervened when she saw they hadn't packed Hannah's underclothes and socks.

"How could we forget that, Hannah?" Mary said.

"Aunt Meg remembers everything," Hannah said.

Tears gushed from her eyes. She rushed to Meg, held her around the knees until Meg lifted her, and said, "You'll be here when I get back promise?"

"I'll be here," Meg said and held back her own tears.

Goodbyes were said for the second or third time. Mary promised to have Hannah back in two or three weeks. As they drove away, Brad's father called out, "Have fun, you two."

CHAPTER 6

B rad followed Meg into the kitchen. "I'm going to miss that rascal," he said. "It's good for her to be with her grandparents, though. They'll spoil her, of course. Did you notice how worried she was that you wouldn't be here when she got back?"

"Yes. We'll have to start preparing Hannah for August when I leave for school."

Silence. Meg clasped and unclasped her hands. Brad stood, paced to the window, looked out, and returned. "I'm going to the basement. Find those journalism course books I promised you. They were used when I bought them, but they'll do unless they've changed the required books by now. They may have. Another way to squeeze money out of students. They may be of some help anyway."

This isn't going to be easy, Meg reminded herself as she sipped a glass of water. He'd be back soon. He'd go to work. What would she do all day? Go jogging; swimming was a thought. She was still sitting at the kitchen table when Brad returned with six books and placed them on the table. "Well, I better get shaved and ready for work. Do you want the bathroom before I go in there?"

Meg shook her head, grabbed one of the books, and opened it. A crude drawing of a nude woman shouting "Down with clothes" startled her.

She thumbed through the book. At the end of every chapter, where there was space empty of printing, someone had drawn one of the crude cartoons, all naked people saying bawdy things. With exaggerated maleness displayed, one man said, "Marriage is okay if you don't get hung up on it."

Meg slammed the book down.

Brad came into the kitchen with a safety razor and shaving cream on his face. "What's the matter? Your face is red."

"It's this damned book. Is this your idea of a joke?" She opened the book, fumbled through the pages until she found the naked man drawing, and thrust it in front of Brad's face.

"Oh, my God, I'm sorry. I forgot about that junk. Some of it is funny, though. I didn't do it, honest. I can't draw an apple. I bought the books used. Whoever had that one before I did must have drawn those things. Do you want me to go through it later and remove all the drawings? I don't think there are any in the others."

An eyebrow lifted as one corner of Brad's mouth curled, almost into a smile, as he looked at the drawing.

Meg felt her mouth curl at both corners. She couldn't stop the full-fledged laugh that escaped.

"I suppose it is funny. I'm sorry I got so angry. Don't tear the pages out. I might miss something important. I mean about journalism, not the drawings."

* * *

She looked doubtfully at her two-year-old swimsuit, a royal blue thing that managed to cover enough to keep her from getting arrested. How long had it been since she had worn it? She struggled into it and saw as much of herself as she could in the bathroom mirror. No doubt she had gained weight, at least five pounds. How long had it been since she jogged? It was time to start it up again, at least while Hannah was gone. Maybe when she got back, they could work out an exercise program. Of course, Hannah already had an exercise program, the way she raced around all day.

Meg took off the suit, tossed it on the bed, and put on sweat clothes that were a faded blue. She locked the apartment door behind her, stretched her leg and arm muscles using an iron railing in front of the building as a bar, and trotted off toward the mall. Jogging had been a part of her life since she returned from Florida. At first, she did it because of the physical benefits. Later, she realized it helped her feel good about herself, about doing something worthwhile.

She made it to the mall by trotting one block, walking one block, then found an unoccupied outside bench and sat huffing and puffing. Her legs and feet ached. It was nearly one o'clock, and she was hungry. *That's it*, she told herself, *run a few blocks, then stuff food in your mouth. You'll lose a lot of weight that way.*

She had the apartment keys, a few dollars, and some change in her pocket. No handkerchief. She wiped the sweat from her brow with the sleeve of one arm, got up, went inside the mall, and scavenged some paper napkins from a McDonald's counter.

Outside again, she wiped away the sweat on her face and watched two small, cotton-white clouds drift across an otherwise deep blue sky. What a beautiful day, even if it was hot. And she had nothing to do. She waited a few more minutes and jogged around the building as she'd seen others do. It was a distance of at least four blocks. A slight, gray-haired woman said hello as she swept past Meg. At the rate she was going, Meg thought the woman might lap her before she got back to the bench. The woman was sitting on the bench when Meg got there and flopped down, breathing hard.

The little woman sat upright like a statue. She was reading a paperback novel, a hot romance, judging from the cover. She folded the page she was reading, tucked the book into a pocket of her light jacket, and said, "Hello. Oh, you're the young lady I ran past a few minutes ago. Just learning to jog?"

"No," Meg panted. "I just haven't done it for a while. I'm out of shape."

"Don't look out of shape to me," the woman said. Her bright, dark eyes shimmered in the sunlight like polished stones. "I don't imagine your young man thinks you're out of shape."

"My young man?" Meg regretted saying it as soon as the words were out. She didn't want to talk with this stranger about the lack of a young man, no matter how friendly and engaging she seemed.

Before the woman could pursue the subject, Meg asked, "Do you jog here often?"

"Every day," the woman replied. "Outside when the weather permits, inside otherwise. It keeps my juices flowing. Now, when I was your age, it was different. My problem then was to try to keep the juices quiet when I looked at a young man, almost any young man. Know what I mean? Of course, you do."

The woman laughed and cackled. "Well, I've been sitting here about five minutes. It's time to jog again. Want to join me?"

"I don't think I could keep up," Meg admitted.

"You set the pace. I like to jog with someone whenever I can. It gets lonely doing it by myself.

My name is Matilda Jones; call me Mattie."

Meg introduced herself, stood, and wondered if she could make it around the mall one more time. She took a deep breath and stepped out. She settled into a comfortable pace but soon was breathing hard. The woman trotted along and talked about her first husband, who had died several years before, and how she had avoided becoming involved with anyone else until years later; her second husband died only a few months after they were married.

"I wasted all those years before I married Harold, my second. I've regretted it, I can tell you. Don't let life pass you by. That's my advice to young people today. Don't let life pass you by."

They had reached the bench, and Meg collapsed onto it.

"I want to do one more lap now, and then I've got to go home and feed the cats," Mattie said. "Nice to meet you. Maybe again sometime."

She was off and running at about twice the pace Meg had set.

Meg was content to sit on the bench and watch the rest of the world go by. People hurried past, went into stores, came out, got out of cars from across the parking lot, went back, got into cars, and drove away. Everyone moving. Yet she was content for the moment to sit there. At least she was breathing normally again.

Mattie's words echoed in her head: *Don't let life pass you by.*

Was she doing that? Of course not. She was getting an education so she could participate in life to the fullest. Who could be more involved than a reporter? You can't expect every moment to be exciting. Ah, but right now *was* exciting. Soon she'd be back in the apartment alone with Brad. *I'd better get back there, shower, and see if I could do something with my hair.*

Don't let life pass you by. The words seemed to bounce off the sidewalk as Meg jogged back to the apartment. She let herself in and raised the sweatshirt over her head. Brad's voice said, "Hey, you might want to wait until you get into the bedroom to undress. If you don't want to wait, I have no objections."

"Sorry," she stammered. "Aren't you home early."

"Yes. I've got an assignment tonight. I am going to a city council meeting to watch a certain character perform. I am doing a feature on the ... uh ... person. Why don't I take you out to eat, then we'll go to the council meeting, and you can watch, try to guess which person is my subject. What do you say?"

"Sounds great. Give me a chance to watch and learn. You don't have to take me to dinner."

"No. But I want to. I've got some reading to do. Be ready about five, okay?"

"I'll be ready." Meg headed for Hannah's bedroom, where she could get out of the sweaty clothes.

She wiped the sweat from her body, using the dry parts of the workout clothes as towels, then put on her worn chenille bathrobe and hoped Brad wouldn't see her as she went to the bathroom. He looked up from a newspaper, smiled, and returned his gaze from her legs to the paper. The cool water cascaded over her body and reminded her of a photo she'd seen of a naked island maiden standing beneath a waterfall. As she lathered her body, she thought of Brad, only a few feet away. Then the old woman—what was her name, Mattie something —popped into her imagination and repeated the words, *Don't let life pass you by*.

"I'll be ready in a jiffy," she said when she hurried from the bathroom. She returned, wearing a pair of white sandals that accented red toenails. Her sleeveless blouse was lavender with a low neckline. Too much, maybe, along with her short shorts.

Brad's eyes wandered up and down her body.

"Shall we go?"

Brad struggled out of the chair and turned sideways as he stood. "There's an Italian place three blocks from here. I've eaten there a couple of times. It is okay. We could walk; it's a nice day."

"I'm all for that."

Outside, a breeze made the heat bearable.

"Not a cloud in the sky," Brad said.

"We probably could use some rain."

Brad agreed. He started to take Meg's hand but changed his mind.

He slowed his pace to match hers.

"If you've never attended a city council meeting, it'll be a surprise. Our great representatives of the people spend more time arguing about potholes, even individual potholes than they do about important things like who is going to stop the mayor from hiring his relatives for city jobs. The way they drag out mundane things, I swear some of them consider the council meetings a chance to escape from home and stay out beyond ten o'clock."

Brad's hand caressed her elbow as he guided her into DeSilvio's Restaurant. Ten tables were arranged in what had been a large living room. Scenes from Rome and Naples were painted on white wallpaper. They were seated near a window as Meg requested.

"I like to watch people go by," she told the waiter.

The picture window looked out on the sidewalk they had just left. Red and white checked tablecloths covered the tables. The smell of garlic, not so strong as to be offensive, blended with the chatter of the early crowd, many of them elderly couples. The waiters were male with white shirts and black vests, most of them young, maybe college students.

"I thought you might know some of these waiters. They look like college students."

"No, I don't see anyone I know. You're right; they probably are college students, maybe home for the summer. I'm looking forward to sinking my teeth into those final two years so I can get a job and get on with my life."

"Don't be in too big a hurry. Enjoy your youth while you can."

"Yes, like you're an old man. I want what you have, a family and a career. Oh, I'm sorry. About your wife, I mean. Still, you and Hannah make a family."

"Not quite. She needs a mother. I've delayed doing anything about it. I don't want to become involved with someone just because of sex. I want someone right for Hannah. My needs come second to hers."

"Why not satisfy both?"

"I hope to, someday. It's strange, all the people, male and female, and yet it isn't easy to find just the right one. I've dated a few times since Dorri left. It never seemed right. I wouldn't be so particular if it weren't for Hannah."

"You must have met a lot of women who would make her a good mother and also be what ... that is ... someone who would fill your needs."

The waiter hovered. Meg ordered spaghetti and meatballs and salad with Italian dressing. Brad ordered the same.

"You wouldn't be eating all that garlic-flavored food if you had a hot date," she said.

"Neither would you. They'll know we're there

at the council meeting."

"Do you take lots of notes when you cover a council meeting, any meeting?" Meg asked.

"I don't cover the meetings themselves anymore. When I did, especially at first, I took copious notes. But a group like a city council, after you've covered it for a while, you know all the names, can almost predict what each of them will say about a given subject. You don't have to take so many notes. I came up with my own brand of shorthand. Nobody else could read it. While we are at the meeting tonight, why don't you take notes as though you were covering it? Good practice. Write your own story; compare it with the one in the paper tomorrow."

"That's a good idea."

Brad reached over with his napkin and wiped what he said was a smear of sauce from her lip.

"Sorry," he said. "Guess I'm so used to keeping Hannah's face clean when she eats ... well ... you know."

"I appreciate it. I wouldn't want to make an entrance at the council meeting with sauce on my face."

The conversation dwindled to a few comments on the food and more talk about the weather. After the bill was paid, the tip was left, and they were outside again; they talked about Hannah.

Brad's hand took Meg's.

"Sorry," he said as he released her hand. "I

guess that's another habit I've acquired while walking with Hannah. I hold her hand, or she'll dash ahead all the time."

"I don't mind. I feel like running ahead myself. It must be the jogging. Here, hold my hand, or I might start running and embarrass us both."

Meg placed her hand in his. It was warm and strong.

They were still a couple of blocks from the apartment. Warmth, like syrup, flowed through her cells, apparently coming from his hand.

"I won't be embarrassed if we run," Brad said. "C'mon."

He trotted, still holding her hand, and she ran to keep up. He stretched his stride and carried her along. Meg felt like a cloud borne along by the forces of nature. Why was he in such a hurry? What about her? She was breathless. From the running or in anticipation of ...

He released her hand in the apartment building lobby. He fumbled with the key and held the door open for her to enter. He let it close behind them and swept her off her feet and into his arms.

He carried her up the stairs, panting by the time they reached his apartment. His perspiration mingled with hers as their cheeks touched. She felt the stubble of his beard against her face. He stood in front of the apartment door. The kiss was clumsy at first, passionate and clumsy. It became an exploration of sensations as his lips and tongue caressed hers.

"What are we doing? What are you doing?" she mumbled, her lips moving against his. He carried her into his bedroom and set her on the bed.

"I don't know where this will lead," he panted. "I know you want a career. I've tried not to get involved. If you want to leave, now is the time. Otherwise, you know what I'm ... what we're doing."

She glanced about the room. A nightstand with a telephone stood near the other side of the bed. A table in the far corner held a computer. There was a closet. His chest heaved as he unbuttoned his shirt. She panted and rubbed her fingertips on his skin. She finished unbuttoning his shirt and slid her hands around to his back. His hands explored outside and inside her shorts. He was ripping his shirt off when the telephone rang.

"Don't," Meg said.

"Damn, I've got to. It might be an assignment, a big story. It'll only take a second."

She collapsed onto the mattress as he grabbed the phone from the nightstand.

"Yes, Daddy's been running, sort of. That's why I'm out of breath. How are you, Hannah?"

The tension drained from Meg's muscles. She lay on her back, legs spread, and closed her eyes.

"It's Hannah; she wants to talk to you."

Meg struggled to a sitting position and took

the phone. "Hello ... Yes, I'm a little out of breath too. We ... your daddy and I just came back from eating at a restaurant. What have you been doing, having a good time?"

Meg listened, at first impatient to end the conversation. Hannah's enthusiasm about all the fun she had cooled her surging blood and brought her back to reality. By the time they finished their conversation, Brad had left the room.

Meg sat on the edge of the bed for a few minutes, straightened her hair, hitched her shorts back up, and went to the kitchen.

"Do we have time, before the council meeting, to make a fresh pot of coffee while I change into something more professional?" she asked.

"No," Brad said. "We'd better get going as soon as you're ready. Get some fresh air." He seemed flustered. "We almost did it, didn't we? I'm sorry."

He avoided her eyes, "It's just that I know you want a career, don't want to get involved, and I don't either."

She silently nodded and slowly turned toward Hannah's room, emerging in a skirt and pumps a few minutes later.

Before Meg could say a word, Brad's big paw grasped her elbow and led her out of the apartment. "Let's go."

There was silence as he drove downtown to City Hall.

CHAPTER 7

B rad introduced Meg to the eight city council members as they came into the council chambers. Meg recorded each name and wondered why there were no women.

She wrote the last name in the notebook when Brad said, "Meg Collins, this is Mayor Ruth Rogers."

The woman was small, an inch shorter than Meg's five feet four, with bright, penetrating eyes. She drew an explanation from Brad why Meg was there. "Welcome to city government, Meg," and took her place on the platform between the eight men.

The large room, paneled with well-polished wood, had a high ceiling that needed painting. Several rows of chairs awaited interested citizens, if there were any. By the time she met the mayor, she had almost recovered from her parched thirst for more of Brad. She began thinking about the story she would write. If only the chairs weren't so close. Brad's arm kept rubbing against hers.

Meg looked around. Not another person at the meeting.

"Is it always like this? Where are the television people?" Meg whispered.

"Usually, but not always," Brad replied. "If the council is going to decide something the public cares about, like rezoning a neighborhood or raising taxes, people show up. There's nothing on the agenda tonight. You won't have much to write about."

The minutes of the previous meeting were read and approved after two of the council members, Tom Clarey, an overweight man with thinning hair, and George Bergman, a man half Clarey's size but with a bullhorn voice, argued about whether the minutes correctly represented their stand on installing a stoplight at Henderson and Clinton Streets. Clarey insisted he was against it, not for it, as the minutes indicated. Bergman insisted Clarey had been for it at the last meeting.

Brad stretched his legs in front of him, sighed, and closed his eyes. Meg took notes, furiously trying to keep up with the heated comments of the two men.

The mayor halted the argument by pounding her gavel and demanding a vote on the minutes. The other six councilmen voted to let the minutes stand as read.

A motion by Bergman to install the stoplight brought forth a rambling speech by Clarey. Meg couldn't determine if he was for or against it. The mayor asked for a motion, and Bergman moved that the stoplight be installed, and it was approved.

A few minutes later, when a councilman was discussing how the fish were biting on the Alliance River south of Naperton, six people, four women and two men marched into the room. They sat in the front row across the aisle from Meg and Brad.

"We're here about the stoplight at Henderson and Clinton," an elderly woman with gray hair and bright makeup said.

"Too late," Councilman Clarey announced. "They already railroaded the thing."

The woman protested and wanted the council to cancel the vote and listen to their arguments.

"You and most of this group, if not all, were here two weeks ago and presented your arguments. The vote stands," the mayor said.

The woman mumbled something under her breath and motioned to the others. They stood like soldiers and marched out.

The rest of the meeting, except for rubber stamps by the council of money already spent, involved a discussion of the stoplight. After three hours, the mayor asked for and got a motion to adjourn.

The councilmen, still arguing, left the chambers in groups of two or three. The mayor stopped and said good night to Brad and Meg.

"Sorry it was such a dull meeting," Brad said. "Hardly anything to report."

"I've got an idea," Meg said.

"Oh."

"I think I know why you were here. Are you doing some kind of feature on Councilman Clarey?"

"You guessed it. He's been on the council for years. He seems to be against everything, yet I think there's more to him than that. I just wanted to see him in action tonight. I'll interview him later, away from here. He's a cab driver. A ride with him and his comments might be interesting."

After they got in his car, Brad asked, "Want to stop for a bite to eat, maybe a drink?"

"No, thanks," she said. "If you don't mind, I'd like to get home and use your computer to write my story while it's fresh in my mind. What I'm planning to do is—"

"No, don't tell me. That's one thing you want to avoid, telling your story before you write it. Once you've told it verbally, it loses its freshness."

In the apartment, Brad went to the bedroom, turned on the light, and swept his hand toward the computer. Meg wondered if he purposely blocked half the doorway so she'd have to squeeze past him to get into the room. She ducked under his arms, looked back with questioning eyes, and turned her back to him.

When he left, she turned on the machine.

Half an hour later, she entered the living room. "Here's my story. Maybe you don't want to be bothered with it tonight."

He seemed to read the story with interest. It described the council chambers, the councilmen, and the room's emptiness in a few paragraphs.

Meg sat across from him, watched him gaze at her legs, pulled her skirt down, and said, "Well?"

He looked into her eyes and said, "Well, indeed. This is good. The same story has been written here many times, by me when I first covered the county board meetings, by others who were new to city council meetings. I've never seen it done better. You've got the touch, baby; you've got it."

Meg's face heated as she lowered her eyes. She couldn't decide if she was embarrassed because he praised her writing or because he called her "baby." What nonsense, calling her baby.

He went to the refrigerator and returned. He handed her a can of Bud Light beer and popped open another one for himself. Meg tasted the beer, slipped her tongue between her lips, liked the taste, swished a portion around in her mouth, and swallowed it.

"Ah." Realizing how it must have looked, she said, "Sorry, I was thirsty."

"Cold beer hits the spot sometimes. I think this sort of thing would be good training for you. Attending the council meeting, I mean. You could do a lot of that, some feature writing, from a child's point of view, Hannah's point of view. Hey, that's a good idea. A series of features about what Naperton offers from a child's point of view: you could take her to places like the zoo and the park, interview her, and show the reader what a child thinks. Want to try it? If it comes off the way I imagine, we could sell the idea to my boss. More money for you for college."

Meg finished the beer and pushed her chair nearer Brad's. "Oh, it sounds wonderful. I get the idea. Only I'd want to question other kids, not just Hannah. You know, names make news. I guess that's stupid, but they do, don't they?"

"Names make readers. Not always news. I like your enthusiasm. Are you always this enthusiastic about things? Wait, I'll get you another beer."

"Okay, but if I drink another one, I'll go to sleep on you," she warned.

"What a pleasant thought."

"What do you mean? Oh, I didn't mean I'd go to sleep *on you.* I just meant ..."

"I know, I'm just kidding," Brad said as he stood, smiled at her, and then went to the kitchen. Meg heard the refrigerator door open and close. She noted his bare feet as he returned.

Does he think I'm silly? Or that I'm trying to suggest sleeping with him? Was I? I love the feature story idea. Why didn't I think of that?

"Here, pleasant dreams," Brad said as he

handed her a beer. "I never thought to offer you a glass. Want one?"

"No, I guess not. When in Rome …"

"I've always drunk beer from the bottle, don't know why. It's colder that way. This is pleasant. I'm glad I thought of it."

Meg watched him stretch his legs out in front of the chair. He put the beer bottle on the floor and stretched his arms toward the ceiling.

"Nothing like a good, relaxing stretch," he said.

"I'm sure," Meg agreed. "Guys have an advantage. You can stretch, slouch, and get as comfortable as you want. Women aren't supposed to do that."

"Why not?"

"If I stretched my legs out like yours, my skirt would be up to my … er … It would be too high."

"So what? You're among friends. I won't tell, I promise. Besides, I like to look at your legs. You already know that, I imagine."

Meg kicked off her shoes and stretched her legs out a little. She glanced down to see what was exposed, then slouched in the same manner as Brad.

"I should go in the bathroom and take off these pantyhose; then, I'd really be comfortable."

"That's one thing I'm glad men aren't saddled with. And bras, what a heat trap they must be. Go ahead, take off your pantyhose; I won't look, maybe just peak a little."

Meg laughed, turned away from him, stripped

off her pantyhose, and tried to get as relaxed as Brad appeared. However, she knew that there was no way she would be relaxed with his maleness so close and inviting. Even taking off the pantyhose made her legs tingle as she touched them. *What would happen if he touched me? Oh, how I wish he would.* She glanced at him and saw him smiling, not at her, but to himself. Brad turned, looked at her, and stopped smiling. He went to his knees in front of her and wrapped his arms around her knees. His hands moved up her legs.

He frantically pulled down her white panties and thrust his face where the panties had been. Her thighs squeezed shut and held him there. Slowly she parted her legs and began to move with an ancient rhythm as he caressed her with his tongue.

She slowly slid down and out of the chair, pushing him away as he tried to maintain contact. Meg wormed her way under him, her lips finding his in a frantic kiss. Her hands fumbled at his shirt. He ripped it from his body, pushed his pants below his knees, and penetrated her moistness.

Later, as they lay exhausted, aware of the floor's hardness, Meg sighed, stretched, and rolled on top of him. He held her and kissed her while he explored her lower back and the roundness below. A sigh escaped. "I'm sorry. I just couldn't resist. We mustn't let it ruin your plans."

Meg didn't answer. Making love had been fantastic, but where would it lead?

The following morning, Brad made coffee, eight cups. He was sitting at the kitchen table when Meg came into the room in her bathrobe. Her hair was a mess.

"I'm sorry about what I, what we did last night. I'll have to leave. I don't imagine you wanted to get so involved with a babysitter—or did you?"

"What do you mean? Surely you don't think I planned this thing, this spur-of-the-moment madness. I hired you to be a babysitter. I didn't plan, well, you know. Ah, would you like some coffee?"

Meg nodded. He set a cup of coffee in front of her. She clasped and unclasped her hands, tracked the lines on the Formica tabletop with one finger ... and cried.

"Was it my fault?" she asked as if she were talking to herself. "Whether you planned it or not, I didn't resist, couldn't resist. So, what do we do now?"

"One thing for sure, I don't want you to leave," Brad said. "Maybe we can avoid each other somehow until Hannah gets back. It'll be easier then, won't it? On the other hand, maybe we should enjoy it until she gets back. What would be the harm? We're both consenting adults."

Meg stood, gulped the remainder of the coffee in her cup, put her hands on her hips, and glared at him. Her bathrobe opened briefly when the belt came loose. She gathered it around her.

"A summer fling. Is that what you think I am? What about Hannah? What would she think of us? She'd know, don't think she wouldn't. She would begin to think I was going to be her mother. What then? No, I'm not going to do that. You'll have to explain to her and think up some story when she gets back. By then, you'll have had time to hire another babysitter. Get an old woman. Maybe one you can resist."

He smiled.

"Why are you laughing at me?" Meg demanded.

"I'm not laughing at you. I ... well, it's ... anyway, I'm not laughing at you. Your eyes sparkle like diamonds when you're angry."

"Ha," she retorted as she turned and left the kitchen.

Meg sat on the bed until the apartment door slammed shut. Brad was gone. She went into the bathroom, stripped, and studied her reflection in the mirror. Meg stayed in the shower until her skin turned pink, got out, toweled off, and went into the living room where she stood for what seemed like several minutes gazing at the spot on the floor where she and Brad ... Meg shook her head, finished toweling off, and hurried into her sweat clothes. A good jog, enough so she'd be too tired to think about Brad, that's what she needed.

The air was damp and hot when she left the

apartment. Clouds hid the sun. She jogged a block, walked a block, and by the time she got to the mall, mist mingled with the sweat on her brow. Meg resisted the urge to find a bench and sit. Instead, she jogged around the mall. The urge to stop, or at least slow to a walk, almost won out. She did manage to jog all the way around, then collapsed onto the bench she had shared with the little old lady; what was her name? Matilda Jones? Yes. *Call me Mattie*, the woman had said.

What was it she had said? Something about living life to the fullest. *Don't let life pass you by—* that was it.

Is that what I'm doing if I leave now? Letting life pass me by? Meg's breathing had nearly returned to normal. Sweat soaked her clothes. Her eyes watered as perspiration irritated them.

"Why are you crying?" Meg recognized the voice.

"Hey ... Mattie, I'm not crying. I just got sweat in my eyes. Sit down."

"Thanks. Sure, you're not crying. Been working out regularly?"

"No, I'm sorry to say. This is the first time since I met you."

"Something's different. You got a new boyfriend?"

"No." She felt comfortable talking to Mattie as if they were longtime friends.

"No, not a new friend. But I'm becoming more

involved than I should with a man. He's older. I've been fascinated with him for some time, and now ..."

"Go on. This is better than any of those books I read."

Mattie moved closer. Bright, alert eyes accented the wrinkles on her face.

"I want to go to college in the fall. That's why I'm working for this guy. The work forces us to be together. I don't want involvement without commitment. I don't know what he wants. There's a child involved. The child was hurt deeply when her mother left, and now I'm sure it will hurt her again when I leave, although I've tried to make it clear to her that I'd be going to college in the fall. I'll leave a little earlier than I planned, that's all."

Mattie took off her backward baseball hat and scratched her head. "Well, if it were me, I'd ask the guy what he wants. What's wrong with that? You've got a right to know. Don't let life pass you by; that's what I always say."

Sunlight broke through a patch of blue in the sky, low and off to the west. Meg held out her hand and turned to Mattie. "It's stopped raining."

"Heck, it never did really rain—just mist. We need a gully washer. Everything is so dry."

Mattie stood. "Want to jog with me?" she asked.

"Sure. I'll try to keep up. Maybe I'll drop a pound or two if I keep sweating."

Mattie set a fast pace to make Meg work at it but not so fast she couldn't keep up. Why not ask him? She did have a right to know his intentions. If he just wanted a summer fling and then let her go out of his life, she had a right to know. Meg wanted marriage, kids ... a daughter like Hannah. Why was life so complicated? Before she realized it, the two women were back at the bench. Meg was breathing hard, harder than Mattie, but the run had made her feel better.

She'd go back to the apartment, get cleaned up, greet Brad with a kiss—well, maybe not. Greet him anyway and bring the conversation around to ask him the question. She could tell him what she wanted. Face the issue directly. Why not? Like Mattie said, "Don't let life pass you by."

Meg glided back to the apartment. Was this what it felt like to fly? The apartment door was unlocked. Had she forgotten to lock it? No. Brad must be home early. She heard voices coming from the kitchen, Brad's and a woman's voice that sounded like a television announcer, robust and precise, each word pronounced precisely. Suddenly, Meg was exhausted. She knocked on the door as she entered the apartment.

Brad's chair scraped on the kitchen floor as he jumped up. "Hello, Meg, this is Dorri, my ... Hannah's mother. Dorri, this is Meg Collins. She's the babysitter I was telling you about."

"You didn't say she was so young and so

athletic. My dear, you must feel awful. You're drenched in sweat."

"Pleased to meet you. Excuse me, I need a shower and out of these clothes."

Meg fled the kitchen. A cold shower didn't help. All the exhilaration she had felt on the way back to the apartment was gone. Dorri was beautiful. Her hair was a shade between platinum and tangerine with every wave in place. Could she be wearing a wig? Meg imagined what a chore it would be to care for such long hair if it was real. And her skin was perfect. Not a blemish. Meg hadn't observed Dorri's figure. However, even sitting down, she looked sleek, like a leopard. Her legs were long, no doubt. But her eyes—that was her one less-than-perfect feature. They were small, dark, and brooding.

Meg returned to the kitchen. Brad and Dorri were silent. It was apparent they had been in an intimate conversation.

"Dorri's going to stay here for a couple of days. She has no place else. She came back to see Hannah. Between pictures. She's been on location in Mexico and had a small part. I can sleep on the couch," Brad added.

"You won't have to sleep on the couch," Meg said. "I'm leaving."

CHAPTER 8

"**N**ow, wait a minute," Brad said. "That's not necessary. Dorri could stay at a motel. She's just going to visit some old friends. She has to be back in Hollywood next week. Why do you have to leave?"

"I could fly to Florida and see Hannah," Dorri said, "but frankly, I can't afford it. That part in Mexico was my first break. I've been keeping my head above water by working other jobs. I'll go for a walk so you two can talk. I don't want to break anything up."

"There's nothing to break up," Meg replied. "I was planning to leave anyway. Brad hired me as a babysitter. Hannah is in Florida, so he doesn't need me."

"But she'll be back in a week or so; what will I do then?" Brad asked.

"I've made up my mind," Meg said with finality after Dorri left the apartment. She was right about Dorri's legs. They were long and slender. Meg would be damned if she was going to stay in the same apartment with his ex-wife.

Maybe he thought they could compare notes or something, the big dummy.

"What the hell's wrong with you?" Brad demanded. "We can work this out. I'll pay for Dorri to stay in a motel. She says she's just hanging on, money-wise, but thinks she'll get a break soon. I doubt it, but I don't want to discourage her."

"No, of course not."

"I suppose this is all about last night. It happened. Why can't you just forget it if it bothers you that much? Hannah will be home soon. We can go on as before. There's still some time left before you go to college. You could learn a lot."

"Yeah, I could learn a lot," she fired back.

Brad took a step toward her as she backed out of the kitchen. "You have your couple of days or whatever with your ex-wife. I'm not going to be around to spoil it. I've got a friend about to have a baby, and I'm sure she'll be happy to have me stay with her and help. It'll be a good experience for me when I find a man who wants to marry me and have a family."

Meg retreated to Hannah's bedroom and stuffed all her clothes into her two battered suitcases, everything she had brought with her. She kept her back turned to Brad, who stood in the doorway. No way was she going to let him see the tears.

"Okay," Brad said. "Okay. You run like a little

kid. I'll hire some old lady to take care of Hannah. She'll be just right for Hannah and me. She'll play checkers with Hannah and teach me to crochet. Won't that be fun!"

"I'm sure it will." Meg wiped tears from her face and resisted the urge to smile at the thought of Brad learning to crochet. She closed her suitcases.

"At least let me take you to your friend's house," Brad said as he stepped aside so she could leave the bedroom.

"No."

She was lugging the suitcases out the front door of the apartment building when Dorri came around the corner. She was walking fast, her head high, her chest out. Probably some sort of exercise to keep her in perfect shape. She looked as if she could run a mile without breaking a sweat.

"Oh, I'm sorry you're leaving. I hope it's not my fault."

I'll bet you're sorry I'm leaving.

"It's not your fault. Brad doesn't need me now, that's all. He can get another sitter when Hannah returns."

Meg knew Dorri saw her wipe another tear from her face. Once she was out of sight, she'd cry like a baby. Was that a smug smile on Dorri's face, or did she imagine it?

Dorri went into the building just as Brittany was coming out. "Are you going on a long trip?"

Brittany asked Meg.

"No, just leaving. You can have Brad all to yourself ... as soon as his ex-wife leaves."

"Why, whatever do you mean?" Brittany said as she walked away. Meg labored to the bus stop like an overloaded wagon. Brad had offered to carry the suitcases to the bus stop. She wished she'd let him. It was several miles to Jan's house. Would she even be home? If she was, would she welcome the unannounced visit? Meg thought to find a telephone, call first. If Jan wasn't home, what then?

By the time she found a pay phone, she was at the mall. Meg fumbled through her purse, recalled Jan's phone number, and dialed. How long had it been since she talked to Jan? At least two weeks. The phone rang several times. Meg was agonizing over what to do next when an out-of-breath Jan answered.

"Hi, Jan, it's Meg. How are you?"

"Hi, stranger," Jan gasped. "I was out in the yard pulling weeds from what is supposed to be a flower bed. How are you?"

"I have a problem. I need a place to stay for a while. Until I find another job. It shouldn't take long; I won't be picky."

"Why, sure, I've wanted you to come over and see our house. We only have two bedrooms. One is fixed for the baby, but we can figure something out. It'll be great to have you here. I've been going nuts staying home waiting for the big event. You can tell me all about what happened when you get here. Where are you?"

"I'm at the Anderson Street Mall. I'll take a bus and be there in half an hour. What about Jerry?"

"What do you mean?"

"Jerry, your husband. Will it be okay with him?"

"Sure, don't worry about Jerry. He'll be glad to have someone else here to listen to my bitching so that he can watch the damned TV."

When a bus finally came, the driver said, "You take the next bus if you want to get to the 200 block of Howard Street."

Mattie jogged by as Meg sat waiting. She was past when she pranced backward until she was opposite Meg and continued to jog in place. "You've been crying; what's the matter?"

"I didn't let life pass me by," Meg said. "Oh, that's not fair. I just need to get away for a while, so I'm going to stay with a friend. Here comes my bus. Keep jogging."

From the window of the bus, as it turned and pulled out of the parking lot, Meg watched Mattie disappear around a corner of the shopping center.

From the bus stop, Meg still had three blocks to walk to Jan's house. The suitcases were as heavy as her heart. Finally, she got close enough to see Jan, as round as a beach ball, sitting on the stoop of her bungalow. Jan lumbered toward Meg as she lugged the suitcases up the walk.

Tears streamed down her face as they embraced.

"We'll dehydrate ourselves if we keep this up. Come in. Tell me what's happening. What about that job you had with your dreamboat? What happened?"

Over a cup of coffee which Jan said she was not supposed to have, Meg spilled out more details than she intended about her relationship with Brad, how his ex-wife came back, and all the complications involving Hannah.

"I'll get another job, find a place to stay, and get on with my life," she said. "I'm going to miss Hannah, though. She's just the daughter I always imagined having."

"Couldn't you visit her?" Jan asked.

"Yeah, maybe, or see her in the park or at the zoo. We went to those places a lot while Brad was at work."

"What about your ambition? Hey, I saw your name with his on that missing-girl story. I would have called and congratulated you, but Mr. Wayne's phone number is unlisted."

"What a surprise that was. I talked to the woman involved without suspecting it would be in the story. I just gave Brad my notes on what she said. He did the rest. I may do some more work for the paper. Brad had an idea about interviewing children and seeing what they think about summer vacation, the park, the zoo, and so forth. I don't suppose his editor will be interested now. Maybe I'll try it anyway."

"Take a tour of the house while I go to the bathroom. I piss every ten minutes. Right now, I'd give up the house, Jerry, and my left arm to be as slim as you are. I'm told it will be over soon. I hope so."

Meg looked at the yellow kitchen table and chairs, the red, green, and white linoleum floor, the cupboards, and the new stove and refrigerator. It seemed awfully cramped. She'd want a larger kitchen. The furniture in the living room was worn. A television set dominated. A computer occupied one corner. She heard the toilet flush, and Jan appeared.

"Don't you just hate this crappy living room? This stuff came from Jerry's old apartment. We'll buy new furniture after the baby comes, but Jerry doesn't make much money. He's an auto mechanic, you know. He wants to go back to school to be an electrician. I don't know how we'll ever be able to afford that unless he goes to night school."

Jan took Meg's elbow, guiding her through a hall by the bathroom and into a small bedroom. Pink and blue balloons clung to the ceiling. A crib was in one corner. The new wallpaper featured cupids and clouds against a sky-blue background. A small single bed had been pushed against one wall.

"You could sleep in here. I hope you don't wake up in the middle of the night and think you're having some weird nightmare."

"This'll be fine, Jan. I'll be out of your hair in a few days."

Meg hauled the suitcases into the bedroom, went into the bathroom, closed the door, and let the silent tears escape.

Later, Jan allowed her to help prepare dinner. Jerry came in, saw her, and smiled.

"It's about time you paid us a visit, young lady. Jan's been wondering how you've been. Seduce that professor yet?"

"Well, I ..."

"I'll explain it to him later, Meg. Just give him a beer from the fridge and head him toward the television or his computer." Jan giggled.

"See?" Jerry said. "Work all day, and this is what I get. She hasn't even kissed me yet."

"You haven't kissed me either, big boy. Not too long ago, you'd be all over me by now."

Jerry took the beer and turned to Jan. "It won't be long before I am all over you again, I hope."

Later, as Meg lay on her back in the small bed, she could hear Jerry snoring and wondered if Jan was awake. She turned onto her side, thinking it would be a long, sleepless night. The next thing she knew, the sound of birds singing woke her. A breeze from the open window caressed her, and a new day was dawning. Today she'd get a new job, maybe two, so she could rent an apartment and save money for college. Meg waited until she was sure Jerry and Jan were through with the bathroom before taking a shower and did as much as she could with her hair.

Jerry was off to work. Jan was sitting at the kitchen table drinking a glass of milk when Meg entered, dressed in blue jeans and sandals.

"Gee, you still have that blouse," Jan said. "Didn't you buy that in California? Yeah, I remember. You said it matched your eyes. Remember how I laughed? Green with white stripes doesn't match anybody's eyes. I guess maybe you meant the green. You going to apply for a job in jeans?"

"Why not? There's a place a few blocks from here where the waitresses wear jeans. That's the name of the place. Jeans Restaurant. We ate there a couple of times, remember?"

"Hey, I saw a 'Waitress Wanted' sign just the other day when I was at that mall over by where your Mr. Wayne lives. You get a job there; he might come in some time. You could see Hannah."

"No, thanks. She'd never understand why I was working there instead of caring for her. I'm going to get a job on this side of town. Plenty of restaurants around here, too."

Meg hadn't noticed before, but there was a sign on the front window of Jeans Restaurant announcing the place was open twenty-four hours a day. Inside she sat at a long counter to the side away from the door and ordered a cup of coffee. The woman who waited on her was large and competent. She was serving six people at the counter and three occupied tables. Meg counted twenty tables, each with its blue and white striped tablecloth and four chairs.

"Who do I see about applying for a job?" she asked when the waitress offered her more coffee.

"You're talking to her," the woman said. "Soon as I get a chance, I'll get you the form. It's a no-brainer. I'd hire a monkey right now."

The woman pushed stringy blond hair back from her face, blew at a strand when it flopped back, and sighed.

"You can start at six tonight if you want. I need somebody I can rely on."

Meg asked if it would be possible to work two shifts a day.

"Honey, if you show up, you can work as many shifts as you want. I'm having a hell of a time keeping waitresses. Too easy for them now, with plenty of tips. They get a little money and go nuts. Go out, get drunk, laid, or whatever, and just don't show up for a while. Then they expect me to take them back. That's a bunch of shit. You ever do this kind of work? Don't matter. I need a body. You'll learn. My name's Rose."

"Will I need a uniform?"

"Don't see no uniform on me, do ya? The only uniform you need is jeans. You're all set. The guy who owns this place is a cheap bastard. He figured he'd get out of buying uniforms by having the waitresses wear jeans. Clever, huh?"

When she reported for work that evening at six, Meg's main worry was learning the menu. She and Jan had been waitresses a couple of times during their trip to California and back, once in Las Vegas, where they gambled away their tips as fast as they got them.

The menu at Jeans turned out to be easy. A meat-and-potatoes place at a family restaurant. The only thing that changed from day to day was the kind of pie on hand.

Meg worked from six p.m. to six a.m. At the end of the first day, despite her ability to sit often in the early morning hours, she was exhausted. Her feet and legs hurt. She sat for half an hour after her shift ended before walking to Jan's house.

As she trudged to Jan's, she tried not to think about it, but images of Brad with Dorri in his arms, images of herself in Brad's arms, of Hannah—they all blurred. She sat on the front steps of Jan's house and blew her nose. Meg knew Jan would spot her red eyes the moment she stepped inside.

Jan sat like a Buddha on one of the kitchen chairs. Meg fetched her a glass of milk.

"How did the job go?" she asked.

"It's not as glamorous as waiting tables in Las Vegas. What was the name of that place?"

"Yancy's, right next to that big casino, Harrod's, wasn't it? Remember how we worked our sweet asses off and lost our money as soon as we got off work—except that you won two hundred dollars once? That money got us home."

"Seems so long ago."

Meg went to sleep but woke up sometime in the afternoon in a sweat. She had been dreaming of Brad and her in bed, in the kitchen on the table, on a beach somewhere, all the time doing exciting things to each other she didn't even know she could imagine. Well, maybe she could imagine them. Like when he carried her upside down with her face against his crotch. He tickled her with his tongue, and she gently chewed on his penis. The motion of his long steps added to the pleasure. Had she dreamed this before?

"You sure get friendly with the kids that come in here," Ellie, one of the waitresses, said during a lull in the evening shifts.

"I'm interviewing them. Rose said it would be okay as long as it didn't interfere with my work."

"Interviewing them? Why?"

"I'm a journalist, or I'm going to be. I'm going to write a story about what they think of summer vacation, their favorite places to go in Naperton, stuff like that. I hope to sell it to the newspaper."

"Gee, a journalist. Like a reporter, huh?"

"Yes," she replied as she hurried away from the counter with another meatloaf and mashed potatoes special.

After writing her first article and rewriting it

several times, she hitched up her nerve and her blue jeans. She went to the newspaper office, where she was directed to the second floor. Meg stood and gawked at the people moving about, the cubicles housing desks, chairs, and computers, and the copy desk in the center of the room.

A young man, in a hurry like most of them, stopped in front of her and asked if she needed help.

"I've got a story I'd like to sell," she stammered.

"Guess you'd better see Ed Grange; he's the bald guy with the mustache in the corner office over there. The guy on the phone."

Meg said thanks and walked around and through the cubicles until she stood in front of the office marked city editor."

The man in a padded swivel chair shouted into a telephone receiver attached to his ear. He stood, still talking. He was taller than Meg expected. His face was an unhealthy pink; his nose was large and red. He continued to talk about something to do with the city council. Finally, he removed the receiver from the side of his face and motioned Meg into the office.

"What do you want?" he said.

"I'm a friend of Brad Wayne's. My name is Meg Collins."

"Meg Collins. Do I know you? Oh yeah, you're the gal who went south with our Mr. Wayne, who has become a cranky bastard lately. Do you have anything to do with that? Never mind. What do you want?"

Meg had been rolling the four pages of her story together until they resembled a tube. She placed the pages on his desk, tried to flatten them out, and put her hands behind her back when he said, "Never mind, I'll get a housekeeper in here to iron them. Your address and phone number are on there somewhere, right? I'll look at the piece later. Busy now. Thanks for bringing it in."

He brushed past her, went halfway across the room, and talked and gestured with a woman who looked twice her age.

Meg had hesitated to take the story to the office, afraid she might run into Brad. Or did she go there because she hoped to run into him? She glanced around the room but didn't see him and wondered which cubicle was his.

* * * *

"I still haven't heard anything from that editor; his name is Ed something, at the paper," Meg complained to Jan two days later. Two days after that, she became a celebrity at the restaurant. She was trying to keep up with the breakfast rush when Rose came into the restaurant waving the latest issue of the *Naperton Daily Press.* She had folded the paper open to page two of the Living section.

"Your story is here, Meg. There is a big headline, and your name is right under it. I think it's great. You got all those quotes right here. But you didn't mention the restaurant."

Meg was carrying three breakfast orders on a tray the size of Texas and didn't dare stop to look. She placed the tray on a table near the first order and said, "That's great, but I can't look at it now. They didn't tell me they were going to use it. And no pay either."

The following day, Jan said, "The famous Meg Collins is living right here in my house. Wait until I tell my daughter. Guess I will have to wait until she's born. There was a call from the newspaper, a guy named Ed Grange. He says he wants you to call him. And ... you had another call from someone named Brad, Brad something, Wayne, I think—yes, that was it—a Brad Wayne. It seems to me I've heard that name."

"How do you suppose he found me?" Meg said and sat down.

"Well, aren't you going to call him?" Jan asked.

"Who? Oh, yes, the editor, Mr. Grange. You bet I'm going to call him. If he thinks I'm going to write for nothing, he's got another thing coming."

"That reminds me, you got a letter today too. From the *Naperton Daily Press*. Maybe that's your pay." Jan picked up the envelope from the kitchen counter and slid it across the table to Meg. She ripped it open.

"Well?" Jan prodded.

"It's a check for one hundred dollars. Gee, I never expected that much. Wow! I better call Mr. Grange."

On the second call, just before Meg had to leave for work, she reached the city editor.

"We want more interviews with kids, and we need a mug shot of you to run with the articles. One a week for the rest of the summer. Can you handle that?"

She gulped and said, "Sure. Thanks for the check."

"That's what I'll pay per article, provided they're all as good as the first one. I need it by Monday of every week. Okay?"

"Yes, oh yes," Meg said.

Back at the restaurant, Meg was still aglow from the conversation with Mr. Grange. She spilled the news to Rose and Ellie and walked on air as she waited on customers—until Brad came in with Hannah. Hannah ran to her and threw her arms around Meg's legs while she was carrying a tray with three orders on it. Meg managed to place the tray on an empty table and lifted her.

"When did you get back, sweetie?" she asked.

"Today. I flew back all by myself. Daddy picked me up at the airport. He said you would tell me why you aren't taking care of me anymore."

Brad caught up with Hannah and eased her from Meg. "We'll have to sit at a table, kiddo, so Meg can do her work. Maybe she'll wait on us, and you can talk to her then. Right, Meg?"

Brad's gaze locked on her eyes. Meg nodded, turned, and picked up the tray. Her knees nearly buckled. She went through the motions of waiting on customers and noted that Brad and Hannah sat in the section Ellie covered.

She was busy on the other side of the restaurant but couldn't resist watching as Brad gestured to Ellie.

"He wants you to wait on them," Ellie said when she returned to the counter.

"Tell him no."

"Hey, you tell him. I'm not getting into the middle of this lover's quarrel or whatever it is. He's got that little girl with him, and you could interview her. I'll take one of your tables."

Ellie took an order from one of Meg's tables before she could protest.

"How did you find me?" she asked as she stood at Brad's table, pencil poised to take his order.

"Don't you like me anymore?" Hannah said.

"Oh, honey, of course, I like you. I'll always like you, love you, Hannah. Your daddy should have explained this to you. It's his job. You should have the children's special. It's roast beef, mashed potatoes and gravy, and green beans. Oh, I forgot, you don't like green beans."

"I'll eat them if you come back. Please."

"We can't talk about this here, Brad. I'm working. Please order."

CHAPTER 9

Meg took the order, including the special for Hannah. Brad ordered steak and eggs, then followed her to the counter. She turned when she got a whiff of aftershave and dropped the order pad. Brad retrieved it. "Please don't mention anything about Dorri being at the apartment. She left before Hannah got back. I don't want Hannah to know she was there and didn't wait to see her."

Meg sagged onto a counter stool. Her sympathy for Hannah spread to Brad, who stood gazing down with sad, imploring eyes.

"I'm glad you told me in time. Of course, I won't mention it."

"Why don't you eat with us? I'll give you some of my green beans," Hannah said as Meg served them. She giggled.

Meg patted her on the head and smiled. "I can't, honey; I'm working."

"Could we talk if we wait until you get off work?" Brad asked.

"I don't get off until six tomorrow morning. You don't want to wait that long."

"Let's wait, Daddy; I can sleep in the car."

"Eat your food, kiddo. Maybe we can talk to Meg some other time."

Hannah cried after eating all her food, and Brad said they had to leave.

"I ate all my green beans, see?" Hannah said.

The next morning, he looked forlorn, sitting in a booth. He said he was going to wait until she got off work.

Meg puttered around but finally had to leave after her replacement arrived. Besides, she was tired and wanted to go to bed.

"Surely you'll talk to me after I got up this early, waited this long."

"Who's with Hannah?"

"Brittany. Hannah stayed with her last night so Brittany wouldn't have to get up so early."

"Of course. We wouldn't want Brittany to get up too early. It might wrinkle her face."

Brad took Meg's elbow and turned her, facing each other. "What was I supposed to do? Have Brittany stay all night?"

"Why not? You can have all your women stay all night for all I care."

"Meg, you're tired. This is unfair. I should have come to where you're staying, talked to you there. What are you trying to do, kill yourself with these long hours?"

"It's none of your business, but I'm earning enough money to go to college. We made a mistake. I'm sorry it involves Hannah, but I was going to have to leave anyway. Now is just as good a time as any. Please leave me alone. Let me go home and get some sleep."

"Let me give you a ride home."

"No, Brad, just go."

Meg walked away, and she heard Brad's feet pounding as he left. Only seconds later, a car sped past. He was angry. So what? She was angry, too. At him, herself, what? All she knew for sure was that she wanted to get to Jan's house and get off her aching feet.

The one thing that kept her going after the confrontation with Brad was the children's interviews. Meg got up in time to go to the park or the zoo in the afternoon and talk to them. Her second article included a photo of her that Jan took. It was surprisingly good. The newspaper must have had someone paint out the background. She peered at the reader as though she were asking another question.

Meg mailed her piece—that's what it was called instead of a story—every Friday and received a check for one hundred dollars the following Wednesday. Her savings account was growing. She was going to make it, and the children and their parents were beginning to recognize her. Meg worried that answers to her questions might be less spontaneous than before. Customers at the restaurant recognized her, too. Their tips were more generous. Even though everything was going her way, she was miserable. When she thought of Brad and his skin next to hers and Hannah's loving smile, she cried, sometimes while she worked.

She always said when people asked about it, "I must have something in my eye."

Every night at work, she checked all the tables to see if Brad and Hannah were there. It had been three weeks since she had seen them. "What are you going to do about it?" Jan said one afternoon after Meg got up.

"About what?"

"You know. Brad and Hannah. You miss them both. Why else would you be bawling all the time?"

Meg knew her eyes were red, but why wouldn't they be? She'd worked all night, hadn't slept well.

"Bawling all the time. I'm not bawling all the time. My eyes are tired. It was a long, smoky night. Something caught fire in the kitchen."

"Uh-huh."

Jan struggled up from a kitchen chair, waddled to the stove, and brought the coffeepot to the table. She topped off Meg's cup and her own.

"You can bullshit other people, Meg Collins, but this is Jan. I know you. You're still mooning about that Brad guy. And if that wasn't enough to bring tears, there's his daughter. You adored her, still do. Back to my original question. What are you going to do about it?"

"Nothing," Meg said.

"Well, stop mooning around and get on with your life."

"I am. I'm working my tail off; I'm writing a weekly column. That's something I never dreamed I'd be able to do this soon."

"You're working your ass off all right; I'll give you that. You've lost those five pounds you've wanted to get rid of for a year or more. Next thing you know, you'll be skinny."

Meg smiled briefly and sighed. She was so tired.

"Speaking of losing weight, aren't you getting close to your due date?"

"Doctor said it should be within the next two weeks. I'm getting anxious and worried. Nervous about how I'll perform during the birth."

"If I know you, you'll swear a lot and do fine. I sure haven't been much help. I thought if I lived here for a while, I could help pay for it by helping you with the housework."

"Pay for it," Jan snorted. "Why would you have to pay for it? My mother will move in and take over as soon as the baby comes. Don't worry about it."

"Where is your mother going to sleep?"

"On the couch, I guess. Don't worry, Meg. The baby will be in our bedroom for a while, at least. We'll work problems out as they arise. Come on, cheer up."

Meg made a mental note to find time to look

for an apartment. She couldn't be the cause of Jan's mother sleeping on the couch.

"I've got to get to the park, get some more interviews with kids. This is the best part of my day. Kids say the most interesting, darling things. A little boy the other day said he wanted me to be his aunt. When I asked him why, he said, 'Because you could do the dishes for me. It's my turn three times a week.'"

Meg's spirits picked up a little as she neared the park. What new questions could she ask? She'd already asked about their favorite things to do during summer vacation, their favorite vacations with their families, and their favorite animals at the zoo.

She had developed a system. She would sit near the swings or sliding board in the park. Usually, many young children were at play, and their mothers were nearby. She'd start a conversation with one of the mothers and explain what she was doing. Most of the time, the mother would call her child or children over. Meg would draw them into a conversation and ask her questions.

Some children were so anxious to get back to playing they wouldn't talk, but others were full of words and loved to let them out.

Today she would ask about any new friends they might have made during the summer. Meg sat next to an elderly woman with gray hair tied in a bun at the back of her head. The hair was pulled so tight Meg wondered if it didn't give the woman a headache.

"Hi," Meg said.

The woman didn't reply. She was thinking of moving on, finding a more receptive person, when she saw Hannah swinging. At the same instant, Hannah saw Meg. A smile burst out on Hannah's face, as radiant as the sun coming from behind a cloud. She was swinging higher than any of the others. She skidded the swing to a stop by dragging her feet in the dust, then ran across the grass to Meg.

"You've scuffed your shoes, and look at the dust all over your legs. What did I tell you? You can't get yourself all dirty, so I must clean you up before your father comes home. Didn't I tell you that?"

When the woman, her pale eyes fierce, finished the tirade, Hannah was in Meg's arms, holding on tight.

"Who are you?" the woman demanded. Hannah continued to cling to Meg.

"I'm a friend of Hannah's. Who are you?"

"Never mind who I am. Come, Hannah, we must go home and scrub you clean before your father gets there."

"She's my babysitter now," Hannah said.

Meg squeezed her a little tighter, and Hannah held on. As their faces touched, Meg felt brave little tears that Hannah must have held back.

"I'm a reporter for the *Naperton Daily Press*," Meg said. "I interview children for a weekly column. Would you let me interview Hannah?"

"Her father works at the newspaper. Do you know him? I suppose I better let you talk to her. If I don't, he'll hear about it. Don't take too long; I want to get back in time for my soap opera."

"Do you mind if Hannah and I take a walk? Children seem to respond best when we just walk and talk casually."

"Yes, do whatever you want, but don't take all day and don't go out of my sight."

"Why don't you come back, Meg?" Hannah pleaded.

Meg hoped the babysitter didn't hear. "What's your babysitter's name?"

"Mrs. Wexley," Hannah said. "She doesn't like me." She frowned, then her face brightened. "Daddy showed me your picture in the paper and read me your story. It was fun hearing what all those kids said. Are you going to ask me some questions?"

"Yes, I am. Are you looking forward to going back to school? Will you be sad when vacation is over? Have you made any new friends this summer?"

"I'll be glad to go back to school. Mrs. Wexley is no fun. I'll go to school all day. Daddy won't need Mrs. Wexley then. I met a boy, sort of. I don't know his name."

"You'll meet new friends," Meg told her as they turned to walk back toward Mrs. Wexley.

"You didn't answer *my* question," Hannah said.

Meg stooped, so she was at eye level and took Hannah's shoulders in her hands. She wiped tears from Hannah's cheeks and one or two from her own.

"I'd love to come back and babysit, but, as I told you, remember, I'm going to college to get a job like your daddy's. We talked about this, didn't we? I had to leave a little earlier than I expected, that's all. We'll get to see each other sometimes."

Meg wished she hadn't said that. She shouldn't suggest things that weren't likely to happen. Hannah would remember. Meg started to rise, and Hannah threw her arms around her neck. She stood, holding the child to her chest. Hannah held on tight.

"My, you're strong," Meg said. "And brave, too, I'll bet. I'll bet you're so brave you can let me put you down, and we'll go back to Mrs. Wexley, and you won't even cry."

Hannah's arms fell away as Meg put her down. They walked back. Mrs. Wexley shouted, "Come, child, we've got to hurry, get back for my program. You can clean yourself up."

Meg turned to avoid Hannah's pleading eyes. Hannah and Mrs. Wexley were half a block away before Meg dared look in their direction. Hannah was several paces behind the babysitter. Mrs. Wexley turned and clapped her hands, and Hannah ran to catch up.

The evening after Meg's column with Hannah's edited quote was published, Brad appeared at the restaurant and sat in Meg's section. She thought of trying to get Ellie to wait on him. Ellie had refused before, though. Meg decided it was her job, and she would do it despite the weak feeling in her knees and the queasy feeling in her stomach. Meg guessed he'd always have that effect on her, even when she finished school and, hopefully, got interested in someone else.

"Hi," she managed to say. "May I take your order?"

"Sit down and talk to me for a minute?"

"No. Waitresses don't sit with customers. We're too busy."

Brad smiled and pointed across the room. Ellie was seated opposite a man, talking and smiling.

"Well, maybe we're not busy right now, but you never know when a lot of customers will come in."

"Sit down, just for a minute, please."

Meg looked at the two occupied tables in her section, realized the customers were not lacking anything and sat down.

Brad's knees touched hers. She edged her legs as far back as possible. It was difficult enough looking at him. Touching was more than she could handle.

"Well?" she said impatiently.

"Why are you doing this? Hannah was thrilled to see you, but she's been unhappy ever since. She did enjoy it when I read your latest column to her. She keeps telling me how much she misses you when Mrs. Wexley is not there."

"At least, I suppose, Mrs. Wexley won't be a temptation for you. Too bad you can't talk Brittany into babysitting full-time. She could move in like I did."

"What is it that's got you so—"

"You don't know, I suppose," Meg hissed. She looked around to see if anyone was listening and kept her voice down. "I know we made a mistake when we gave in to *our* desires—just a weak moment."

"You could stay there the rest of the summer. You wouldn't have to be working here. What about your education? You were going to study with those books. Pick my brain."

"Ha, my education. I'd be putty in your hands. I'd never get to college. Be your babysitter for the rest of my life. No thanks."

Meg slid out of the booth and held her order pad at the ready. "Are you going to order or not?"

"No, I don't have time. Brittany is with Hannah, and I promised I'd be back in an hour."

"Maybe Brittany could cook for you, or doesn't she do that kind of thing?"

"Hannah and I have already eaten, thanks. I don't think Brittany could boil an egg. Your columns are good, but you should plan to have a photographer with you. Next time, get shots of the kids. Have a nice life."

Brad slid out of the booth and left. Meg sat

down again.

She rubbed the back of her hand against her eyes and looked around to see if her tables needed service. They didn't for the moment. Was she throwing away her only chance at happiness by refusing to go back to Brad's?

My only chance at happiness? Ridiculous. I'll meet men at college, young men, babies really. I want Brad, but I will not be just a babysitter.

The next day, Meg sat on a bench at the zoo and talked to two women. They called three children from the fence surrounding the monkey compound.

One little girl began talking to Meg. Her small face, dotted with freckles, was animated as she talked. A top tooth was missing. Meg was startled when a camera flashed her face.

Her next interviewee was a little boy. His dark eyes glistened in his freckled face as he talked and gestured. In answering one of her questions, he said, "I think school stinks. I wish I didn't have to go back."

He was the brother of the little girl Meg had just interviewed. There was another flash.

Meg turned and saw Brad. She stood, dropped her notepad, and turned to the boy. "Thank you, Tommy; you can go now."

The boy raced away.

"What are you doing?" she demanded. She stooped and picked up her notepad. When she straightened, her fisted hands were on her hips.

"I'm here to look at the monkeys too?" Brad said.

"Don't get too close. They'll put you inside. What are you doing?"

"I'm taking pictures of your interview subjects. I'd forgotten how much I enjoy doing this."

"I didn't know you were a photographer."

"There's a lot of things you don't know. You could learn a lot from me, about journalism, I mean. We never did get started on all those books I gave you. They're still in the living room on the floor."

"I'm so busy with the column and the restaurant that I wouldn't have had time to read them anyway. I'll continue my education this fall. I've got to interview a couple more kids and get to the restaurant."

"You're getting invaluable experience writing this column. Did you know the university has extension courses here in Naperton? You could go to those classes."

"I know. But they don't have any journalism classes this coming semester. I already checked."

"What do you need with journalism courses? Working like this and with me teaching you, you couldn't get a better education."

"Brad, just forget it. I'm not going to make a career of being your babysitter. Or your lover. I want something more. Now let me get on with this so I can ..."

Meg sat down again, and Brad moved back.

She avoided looking at him. She interviewed two more children, and Brad took pictures. When she finished, he took the names in the order of the kids he'd photographed. Meg watched as his strides traveled across the grassy area to the parking lot. Was that her life walking away? He waved from his car. She turned away.

Meg was busy for the first part of the shift at the restaurant. By two o'clock in the morning, the pace had slowed. Meg sat at a table with Ellie and relaxed. "It's good to give my feet a rest. My brain, too. Food orders race through my mind when I get home after working here. Does that happen to you?"

"Naw, not anymore." Ellie got up to wait on a young man who slid into a booth in her station.

Meg's mind returned to the zoo, where it had been half the time since she got to work. Apparently, Brad didn't care enough about her to offer something besides a babysitting job and being his lover. What did she want? Not that. She wanted to be his wife, to take care of him and Hannah. She also wanted a journalism career of her own. She was well on her way to a career. Did she want to throw that away to be with Brad? No, she just would not do it.

Still, images of Brad's body joined with hers tormented her. Just one night. Was that all she would ever allow herself to have?

CHAPTER 10

"**W**hew, I'm glad that's over," Meg said.

"What's over? You write another column?" Jan slumped in the kitchen chair across from Meg, away from the table, her legs spread, her hands on her enlarged stomach.

"All this university paperwork. I'm all set for the fall semester. Every aggravating detail is taken care of—I hope. How are you feeling?"

"Like a stuffed pork chop. Yesterday the doctor told me it'll be any time now, no more than a week. Means nothing to him, but it seems like a long time to me."

"I've got to get to work, and tomorrow I'm going to find a room to rent. When's your mother moving in? Surely it will be soon."

Jan waved a hand in the air.

"Stay, Meg. Ma's not coming until I go to the hospital. You can find a room then if you insist. Help me up before you go. I get in a position like this, and ...."

Meg laughed and extended a hand.

"Go ahead, laugh. Someday you'll be in this

condition if you ever stop mooning over that Brad guy. Sure, he's long and lean, has brown curly hair and eyes that bore right into your crotch, but what the hell, settle for an average guy and get on with your life."

"My, Mrs. Turner, how you talk. It must be your condition. I've got to go."

Meg settled into taking orders at the restaurant, placing them on the spindle at the kitchen counter, serving coffee and other drinks, and trying to avoid Jack Archer. She hadn't told Jan about Jack. He was a regular customer, always sat at one of her tables, and was putting the hit on her.

It was nice, in a way, at first. Nice to know someone found her attractive. But he was so insistent. She had turned down his requests for dates several times. He just wouldn't quit.

He was at table nine now, watching her every move, waiting, ready to pounce. Meg avoided serving him as long as possible. Finally, she stood in front of his table, said, "Good evening," and asked if he was ready to order.

"Yes, Meg Collins, I'm ready to order. I'll have a dozen of your lips, maybe two dozen hugs, and a date for your next night off, which is?"

"How do you know my last name? I never get a night off, Jack, so give it up. C'mon. Order, please. We're busy tonight."

"Doesn't look busy to me. I know a lot about you. You could sit with me like you did that guy the other night. Who's he, your sugar daddy? I get jealous just thinking about it."

Meg turned and started to walk away.

"Okay, okay. I'll order. I'll have the usual."

"The usual? What's that?"

"Well, you know, kisses and all that stuff. No, don't leave. Guess I'll have the meatloaf special, coffee, and maybe some dessert later. In the meantime, I'll just sit and watch the tremendous sway of your lovely hips as you promenade about the place."

Promenade? Do I promenade? Until it got busy again, Meg was conscious of how she walked. Jealous? Was he jealous of the way she sat with Brad? If Brad ever came in again, she'd sit with Jack, hoping it made Brad jealous. What a juvenile idea.

Eventually, she did get busy enough to forget Jack and her "promenading." He left after two more cups of coffee and apple pie à la mode.

Business slowed, and Meg took the opportunity to look at the "For Rent" ads in the latest edition of the *Naperton Daily Press*. Three rooms within a few blocks of the restaurant were for rent. She hated the idea of moving again. It felt so final like she was losing all the connections in her life—Jan and Jerry—and the connection to Brad and Hannah. Well, at least for the rest of the summer, she'd visit Jan and the new baby as often as possible.

* * *

Meg sat at a picnic table in a shaded area near the edge of the park, away from the playground, and nibbled on a chicken salad sandwich. It was all that was left of a picnic basket she'd prepared for herself. Jan had talked about joining her but backed out at the last moment. A few white clouds drifted, and a cooling breeze teased the heat. Meg heard the muted sounds of children at play on swings and slides across the grassy field. She purposely left her notepad and pencil behind. She hadn't spent any time at the park lately, except when she worked. She wasn't fooling herself. Meg hoped to see Hannah ... and Brad. What good would it do? What harm? Couldn't she hope to see a child she loved without it becoming a big deal?

Sitting on the park bench became uncomfortable. Meg felt like putting her arms on a table and using them as a pillow. But she was afraid to sleep. And dream. Dream of being on a blanket spread out on the grass at the park. Hannah would be playing where they could see her—swinging. The clouds would drift by. Brad would kiss her. Meg shook her head. Time to get going, time to go to work. She ate the rest of the sandwich and put residue from the picnic in a garbage can. Then she saw Hannah race along a walk leading to the swings.

What was Hannah doing in the park alone? Then she saw Brad, strolling along behind— with a woman. Damn Brittany. She walked as though she were balancing a book on her head and held Brad's hand.

Meg hurried away and didn't look back until she was behind a tree. Hannah was swinging. Brad and Brittany sat at one of the picnic tables. Were they still holding hands? She couldn't be sure, but it was time for her to go to work.

*

* * *

It was a little after one before business slowed, and Meg had time to think of Brad and Hannah. Brad? Could he really be thinking of Brittany as a mother for Hannah? As a bed partner? Well, he could just sleep with her for all she cared. It was Hannah she was concerned about. Brittany would make a terrible mother. Or was Meg just jealous? Maybe Brittany would make a better mother than she thought. No, it couldn't be. Brittany didn't like children; anyone could see that.

"Hi, mind if I join you?"

Meg jumped at the sound, and Jack Archer leered. He wasn't as tall as Brad, wasn't as handsome. She didn't even know what he did for a living.

"Sit down. I've been resting here for a few

minutes. I'll have to get going again soon. What do you want?"

"You know what I want."

Meg didn't reply. She thought of Brad. Was he making love to Brittany? Maybe she should get even, start dating Jack.

It wasn't exactly a date, but Meg agreed to go for a walk in the park with Jack. She hoped Brad would be there, get jealous, and even confront her because she was with another man. Brad was there, sitting alone on a bench near the swings. Hannah was swinging by herself. Meg's heart swelled as if it would break, seeing her so alone.

"Meg," a familiar voice shouted.

"Hello, Brad. This is Jack."

Brad mumbled, "Glad to meet you."

"Isn't she something?" Jack said, nodding toward Meg. "She writes a column for the newspaper."

"Really?" Brad said.

"I'm a salesman," Jack said. "I can sell anything. Meg here didn't want to go out with me, but hey, I talked her into it. I sell siding, house siding. Harder to sell in the summer when it's so damned hot, but I sell it."

"It's such a nice evening," Meg chimed in, "I thought we'd go for a walk here in the park. Oh, there's Hannah."

"Seems kinda hot to me to be walking, but whatever the little lady wants," Jack said. "Hey,

Meg, where ya goin'?"

Meg ran toward the slide and got there just as Hannah swept to the ground. She picked her up and swung her around. Hannah screamed with delight.

It was worth walking with Jack, she decided. She wiped tears from Hannah's little cheeks. It seemed as if they were always crying whenever they met. Meg knew it was selfish to bring Jack to the park, hoping she'd see Hannah and Brad. She had created another tearful parting to hold Hannah once more.

When they returned to the bench where Brad and Jack were sitting, Jack said, "Hey, I didn't know you had a kid."

CHAPTER 11

Meg had created the problem and had to figure a way to get out of it.

"Look, Jack, the restaurant is busy. Come back a little later, around nine o'clock. I'll talk to you then. You must understand. We're not an item just because we went for a walk."

"That's not like a roll in the hay, then." Jack harassed.

"Jack!" she remarked.

"I gotcha, I gotcha. I'll be back unless I find another girl."

Meg sighed as he left. He talked loud enough that she was afraid everyone had heard. Rose, the boss, raised her eyebrows when Meg came to the counter to get another order.

"What can I do? He thinks I'm his girl just because we went for a walk."

"I don't care what he thinks. At least you got rid of him."

As it neared nine o'clock and business slowed, Meg regretted she'd told Jack to come back. She sat at the counter and sipped a cup of coffee.

The door jangled open, and she turned to see where the newest customer was going to sit. She spilled coffee. It was Brad—and Hannah. It was late for Hannah to be eating supper. Friday night. At least she didn't have to go to school the next day.

Brad and Hannah went right to a table in Meg's section. Hannah waved enthusiastically and wiggled in her chair. Meg waved and went to the other two tables and checked to see if the customers needed anything. When they didn't, there was nothing to do but wait on Brad and Hannah.

"Good evening," she said, hoping she sounded professional as if it were just another table to wait upon. "How are you, Hannah?"

"Daddy has got something to ask you," Hannah said with her six-year-old brand of delightful enthusiasm.

"Do you want to order now?" Meg asked. Her hands shook as she held the order pad at the ready. Surely Brad noticed. His eyes locked on hers. She couldn't look away.

"Well, Daddy, go ahead."

"Look, kiddo, I don't know what you're talking about," Brad said without taking his eyes from Meg. "I let you stay up this late; I agreed to bring you here for dessert, that's all."

Brad was talking so loudly that everyone in the place could hear. What would Rose think?

"Daddy's going to ask you to marry him,"

Hannah shouted.

Meg looked down at her shoes. She just knew every ear in the place had heard. Probably every eye in the place was on her at the moment. She glanced back at the counter. Rose was watching, and the cook had come from the kitchen. Meg scanned the room. She was right—everyone was watching.

"Hannah, I ...," Brad started to say. "This is not the place. Besides, I told you. Meg doesn't want to get married. She wants to go to college."

"Can't she go to college if she gets married?" Hannah innocently asked.

"I'm sorry, Meg. This isn't very comfortable. Hannah got this idea in her head and just won't let it go," Brad apologized.

Then he turned back to his daughter. "Hannah, well, yes, maybe, but how could she take care of you if she went to college?"

Meg forgot the staring eyes and the attentive ears. She thought for a second and explained, "I could go to night school. The university conducts extension courses right here in Naperton. Oh, you know that. Maybe they will have journalism courses later."

A voice from the far corner of the room, a man's strong voice, said, "Go ahead, Mister. Ask her to marry you so I can get some service here."

The restaurant fell silent, and Meg felt faint. Brad wiped his forehead, stood, took the order pad and pencil from her, and took her hands in his. "Will you marry me, Meg Collins?"

"Yes," she whispered. "Yes," she said again, louder this time.

Hannah jumped from her chair and threw her arms around Meg's knees. Applause burst from the customers and employees in Jeans Restaurant.

Finis

ACKNOWLEDGMENTS

My sister, Jeannie, constantly supported my efforts to fill the roles of publisher, author, and creative director of Bancroft Mysteries, LLC.

Ginny, Carol, Janet, Bob, Benjamin, and Russel are friends who were willing to read and reread manuscript drafts and offer invaluable feedback.

Tamian Wood, the cover art designer of Beyond Design, provided Cyn Castle Romances with visual pizazz.

Jean Marie Stine, my mentor and original publisher of Bob Liter's books supported my goal of independent publisher.

Mom and Dad, Bob and Lillian Liter, inspired me to follow a path of passion and adventure, to celebrate their legacy and leave mine.

To all, my deepest appreciation.

Martie Liter Ogborn

ABOUT THE AUTHORS

 **Bob Liter (1923–2008)** a Drake University graduate, earned his journalism degree in 1947. He began a long career as a reporter, columnist, and copy editor. After he retired from the *Peoria Journal Star*, he wrote the Bancroft Mysteries, in the early 2000s. He also wrote a series of contemporary romances from the 1980s under the pen name Cyn Castle.

 **Lillian Hyde Liter (1931–2008)** married Bob Liter on March 4, 1950. Lillian is the inspiration for Maggie Atley in the Bancroft Mysteries, especially in the charming way she deals with the protagonist Nick Bancroft, a self-proclaimed "male chauvinist piggy," who resembles Bob Liter with his wit and bodaciously gutsy approach to life.

 **Martie Liter Ogborn** is celebrating her parents' legacy and leaving her own by independently publishing and writing sequels to Bob Liter's manuscripts. Her latest project is to personify the pen name Cyn Castle created by her father. The rereleased novels bring to life the sex and sizzle of the '80s. The Cyn Castle Romances and the Bancroft Mysteries are set south of Chicago along Route 66 in a decade filled with equal parts nostalgia, desire, and mystery.

NOTE FROM THE PUBLISHER

Bancroft Mysteries, LLC, was established in 2022 to distribute mysteries Bob Liter wrote and to publish romances authored by Bob Liter under the pen name Cyn Castle.

The entertaining manuscripts, written in and about the 1980s, are as true to Bob's original work as possible to preserve that particular time and place in history while providing the reader with an enjoyable reading experience.

Bancroft Mysteries
Murder by the Book
August Is Murder
Death Sting
Point of Murder
And the Band Played On
Love and Other Sports
Murder Inherited

Cyn Castle Romances
My Dream Lover
Rainy Day Lover
Danny Boy
Nola
Eva
Rachel's Confession